LADY GUNSMITH

4

Roxy Doyle
and
The Traveling Circus Show

Books by J.R. Roberts
(Robert J. Randisi)

Lady Gunsmith series
The Legend of Roxy Doyle
The Three Graves of Roxy Doyle
Roxy Doyle and The Shanghai Saloon
Roxy Doyle and The Traveling Circus Show

Coming Spring 2018!
Lady Gunsmith **Book 5**

The Gunsmith series
Books 1 - 200

Angel Eyes series
The Miracle of Revenge
Death's Angel
Wolf Pass
Chinatown Justice

Tracker series
The Winning Hand
Lincoln County
The Blue Cut Job
Chinatown Chance

Mountain Jack Pike series
Mountain Jack Pike
Rocky Mountain Kill
Comanche Come-On
Crow Bait

For more information visit:
www.speakingvolumes.us

LADY GUNSMITH

4

Roxy Doyle
and
The Traveling Circus Show

J. R. Roberts

SPEAKING VOLUMES, LLC
NAPLES, FLORIDA
2017

Roxy Doyle and The Traveling Circus Show

Copyright © 2017 by Robert J. Randisi

ISBN 978-1-62815-740-6

PART ONE

BLACKHAWK

Chapter One

Blackhawk, Colorado

Roxy Doyle had never been to Blackhawk Colorado before. Denver, yes, which was about 50 miles away, but not Blackhawk. However, a recent telegram from Robert Pinkerton, of the Pinkerton Detective Agency, changed that.

She had done a job for the Pinkertons in San Francisco, and Robert had promised to do what he could to locate her missing father, who she had now been searching years for. The telegram found her in New Mexico, where she had tracked down a rumor about her father that turned out—like most of them—to be untrue. But she could not afford to ignore any of them.

Pinkerton's message told her there was a good chance her father could be found in Blackhawk, Colorado, and she immediately headed there.

Now, as she rode into town, she saw all sorts of activity on the main street. Mostly wagons, drawn by two horses each, with people hanging out of them, waving to spectators. She couldn't ride the rest of the way because the street was blocked, so she dismounted and stepped up onto the boardwalk.

"What's all the fuss?" she asked a woman.

Faded and middle-aged, the woman did a double take when she looked at Roxy, and took an instant dislike to the beautiful, younger woman—something Roxy was used to.

"Circus is in town," the woman muttered.

"They're on their way to Denver, but they decided to stop here first," added the man with her. He was eyeing Roxy in an entirely different way than his wife had. And as he did so, the faded woman jabbed her sharp elbow into his ribs.

"Thanks," Roxy said.

Just what she needed, she thought, crowds of people a circus would bring to town.

She had to wait for the wagons to finish their parade down the street before she remounted and went looking for a hotel and livery. These tasks were the drudgery of being in a new town, but they had to be done.

Afterward, she went in search of a meal and a beer, hopefully finding someplace where she could get both. She didn't want to have to go to a saloon. That was usually just looking for trouble, a beautiful woman like her in a saloon with drunk men.

Luckily, she found a little café that had empty tables, where she was able to relax and get a chicken sandwich and a mug of beer.

"Just get to town?" the older waitress asked, as she set down the plate and mug.

Roxy noticed she had a way with waitresses, for some reason. Especially older ones, who wanted to take care of her.

"That's right," she said.

"Are you here for the circus?"

"No," Roxy said, "I didn't know anything about it until I rode in just a little while ago, behind their parade."

"What brings you to town, then?" the woman asked.

"Right now," Roxy said, "this sandwich and this beer."

The waitress smiled. "I'm sorry. I'm keepin' you from eatin'. Go ahead, enjoy."

"Thank you."

And she did. She'd been riding for some time, eating on the trail, and the sandwich and beer were going down extremely smoothly.

Other diners came and went while Roxy took her time over her meal. The men looked her over and their women snapped at them for it, sending hot, hateful looks Roxy's way.

Before long, there was only Roxy and a family of three— mother, father and 5 or 6-year-old son—in the place. The young father was clearly in love with his wife, for he hardly looked Roxy's way.

And for that reason, he attracted Roxy's attention. Also the fact that he was wearing a badge.

When the waitress came over to see if she could get Roxy anything else Roxy asked, "Who's that young feller over there, the sheriff?"

"Andy? No, he's the deputy around here. And that's his wife and sweet son."

"Nice looking family," Roxy said.

She'd probably never have a family like that, she thought. Not with the upbringing she'd had, and certainly not until she was able to find her father, famed bounty hunter

Gavin Doyle. For that reason she felt herself being envious of the young wife, and interested in the deputy. She knew she could probably have him if she wanted to take him away from his family.

Chapter Two

Roxy finished her sandwich and beer, and then paid. But as she left she looked over and saw the young deputy look at her, and then quickly look away. She had a smile on her face as she went outside.

She had planned to go and see the sheriff, but now she decided to wait for the deputy to finish his lunch with his cute family and go back to work.

Until then, she decided to take a walk around town. It was much too early to go to her room and sleep. She was so tired she might not wake for days. Maybe, just maybe she'd see her father.

Not likely, but she started walking.

***

The circus people had put posters up all over town, advertising their show. Apparently, they had lion tamers, acrobats, clowns . . . and a sharpshooter.

She found the poster featuring the sharpshooter and read it. His name was Bill Weatherly, and the poster declared him to be the finest shot in the world. She was curious. The best shot she had ever seen was Clint Adams, the Gunsmith, the man who had trained her. And Roxy felt that she was second only to him, which was why she was called Lady Gunsmith.

She wondered what a man like Bill Weatherly had done before joining a circus. Maybe a man who lived by his gun would know something about Gavin Doyle?

The first performances of the circus were supposed to be tomorrow, so she still had a day to kill.

She walked for a couple more hours, all it took for her to see the entire town of Blackhawk. It seemed to have six streets north to south, and three east to west. Not a large town, but from all appearance, a growing one. New buildings were being erected on several streets, and land seemed to be undergoing plowing and clearing.

When she returned to the main street she decided it was time to go to the sheriff's office.

***

Blackhawk's main street was called Main Street, and the sheriff's office was there. She had only to walk a block to reach it.

She entered without knocking, and the man at the desk looked up at her. She was disappointed that it was not the young deputy, but the sheriff, himself. An older man, she nevertheless recognized the look on his face as he regarded her.

"Well, well," the white-haired man said, "when did you get to town?"

"Just today," she said,

"And what can I do for you, little lady?" he asked. "Are you with the circus?"

She laughed. "No, I'm not. I'm here looking for my father."

"And who might that be?"

"Gavin Doyle."

"Doyle. I heard he was dead."

"I don't believe that."

"Do you have any proof?"

"No," she said, "but I've been looking for him for years, following rumors."

"There are always rumors, little lad—"

"Don't call me that! I'm Roxy Doyle, his daughter. If he was dead, I'd know it. I'd . . . feel it."

"Wait a minute," the sheriff said, "I know who you are now. You're the one they call Lady Gunsmith."

"I'm not here for any trouble, Sheriff," she said. "I'm just following up on some information I received."

"That your dad is here, in Blackhawk?"

"Yes."

"I'm sorry, but not that I know of."

"Then maybe he's on his way here," she said. "I intend to wait."

"And cause no trouble?" he asked.

"That's the plan."

"Then I don't see any reason you shouldn't stay," the sheriff said. "Take in the circus while you're here."

"Thanks," she said. "I might do that."

"And if you need anything," he added, "let me know. I'm Sheriff Kyle Marks."

"Sheriff Marks."

At that moment the office door opened and the young deputy entered. Roxy noticed two things: how handsome he was, and how young.

"Sorry I'm late, sheriff," he said. "I had lunch with Lily and Sam."

"I don't care about your wife and kid, Andy," the sheriff said. "I just expect you to get here and do your job."

"Yes, sir." The deputy looked at Roxy, who smiled back at him.

"Oh, yes, well, Roxy Doyle, this is my deputy, Andy."

"Nice to meet you," Andy said.

"You, too, deputy."

"Stop starin', you idiot!" the sheriff said. "Go and make your rounds."

"Yessir." He tipped his hat to Roxy. "Ma'am."

"I'll walk out with you, Deputy," she said. "I'm done here."

Chapter Three

Outside the office she said to him, "He's not a very nice man, is he?"

"No, he's not," Andy said.

"He didn't even tell me your last name."

"It's Starrett," the deputy said. "I'm Deputy Andy Starrett."

"I saw you and your family at lunch, this afternoon," Roxy said.

"I saw you, too," Starrett admitted.

"I thought you might have," Roxy said. "Your son is adorable."

"Thank you."

"And your wife, she's very pretty."

"Yes, she is."

"Does she satisfy you?"

"W-what?" he asked. "Did you say something?"

"No," she said, quickly. She was embarrassed. He was so young and handsome, and she'd been on the trail along time. Would she ever have time to build a relationship with a man like this? Make a family?

"Look at you." She touched his face, stoked his cheek. "You're so handsome."

"Wha—I— "His face turned beat red. "I—I have to make my rounds."

She dropped her hand.

"Of course you do," she said, "You're a good deputy. Don't worry, we'll see each other, again."

"I—uh, okay," he said.

"Go ahead, handsome," she said. "Do your job."

He turned and walked away. She smiled, then shook her head. She was being bad. Why dally with a married young deputy when she had things to do?

Better things.

***

She decided not to wait for the next day to visit the circus. After two days in the hotel, her money would be gone. She wouldn't be able to buy any food, or pay for her horse's care, and she'd end up on the street.

The circus had a sharpshooter, and she thought maybe they'd want another one. But then she saw a poster sponsoring a sharpshooting contest. Anyone who could beat the circus sharpshooter would win $500. That would be plenty to fund her search for her father if, indeed, she didn't find him in Blackhawk.

Folks were to sign up for the contest on the circus grounds outside of town, so she headed there.

***

When she got there she saw the tents going up, people running around doing their job to get everything set for the next day.

11

Off to one side was a woman seated at a table with a sign that said: SHARPSHOOTING SIGN-UP. She walked over to it.

"Hello, there," the woman said. "Wanna sign up?"

"I sure do."

"There you go," The woman turned the sign-up sheet around toward Roxy, who wrote her name. There were at least a dozen other names on it.

"Lots of people turning out," she said, handing the sheet back.

"Yeah, there are . . . Roxy," the woman said, reading her name. "Five hundred dollars is a big reason."

"What do you do here?" Roxy asked.

The woman looked up at her. She was in her forties, very pretty, with lines in the corners of her eyes and mouth that did nothing to take away from that fact.

"Oh, a little of this, a little of that," the woman said. "Lots of paperwork. I fill in when somebody's sick. I've even been a clown."

"A lady clown?"

"Well," she said, "nobody knows I'm a lady when I'm dressed up as a clown." She put her hand out. "Jillian. Just call me Jill."

"Roxy." They shook hands.

"You know how to use that gun?" Jill asked.

"Yes."

"And a rifle?"

Roxy nodded.

"Well," Jill said. "Bill Weatherly's pretty good."

"I think I've got a fair shot at winning the five hundred dollars," Roxy said.

"I wish you luck, then," Jill said. "Be here tomorrow at eleven. But come for the opening at nine."

"I wouldn't miss it, Jill."

"You know," Jill said, as Roxy turned to leave, "you could make a lot more money trading on your looks, instead of relying on your gun."

"You really think so?"

"I know so," Jill said. "You're gorgeous."

"Thank you."

"I was pretty in my time," the woman went on, "but never like you."

"I think you're very pretty, now," Roxy said.

"Thanks," Jill said, "maybe we can have a cup of coffee together some time."

"I'd like that," Roxy said.

"See ya."

Roxy nodded, and walked away.

Chapter Four

Roxy sat in her room and counted her money. She had enough for one more night, and a couple of meals. If she didn't win the sharpshooting contest she was going to have to get a job.

She remained in her room, not having enough money for a saloon, and not wanting the trouble a saloon usually brought.

***

In the morning she had a cheap breakfast at her hotel before walking through town to the circus grounds, carrying her rifle. Many people, mostly women and children, and a few families, were already there, inside, or in line to pay to get in.

She stood in line and as she got to the front the clown accepting the ticket money said, "You go in free, girlie."

"Why?"

"Jill told me to expect you," the clown said. "You signed up for the contest, right?"

"Right."

"Then you get in free." The clown bowed and waved her in.

She went through the gate. As she did the clown shouted, "Contestants gather outside the big top!"

She heard a calliope playing somewhere on the grounds, heard children laughing with joy or crying. She knew some children feared clowns. She hadn't been too crazy about them herself when she was a kid.

There were jugglers and acrobats working on the grounds, delighting people, and she could hear lions roaring.

"You made it!" someone said.

She turned and saw Jill walking toward her. She was dressed as Roxy was, a shirt, trousers and boots, but Jill's pants were much tighter, showing off what powerful thighs and calves she had.

"You told me to come early," Roxy said.

"So I did. How about we get that coffee now? You've got time before you have to be at the big top for the contest."

"Is there a place for coffee?" Roxy asked.

Jill smiled.

"I'll take you where we carnies go."

"Carnies?" Roxy asked.

"This used to be a carnival, before we graduated to being a full blown circus. Some of us still think of ourselves as carnies. Come on."

She led Roxy across the grounds to a tent back where the public was not allowed.

"How do you take it?"

"Black."

Jill got two black coffees, then led the way to a table and bench where they could sit. She handed one cup to Roxy.

"Thanks."

"I know who you are," Jill said.

"You do?"

Jill nodded.

"Lady Gunsmith."

"How do you know that?"

"Well," Jill said, "I've heard of you, heard your name. I also saw you once."

"When was that?"

"A few years back, when I was taking a break from all this," Jill said. "I rode off on my own, found myself in a town called Red Rim, Nebraska. That was where I saw you."

Red Rim. Roxy remembered.

"You killed two men in a fair fight, right in the street. I never saw anything so thrilling."

"Thrilling?"

"Hey," Jill said, "a woman taking on two men, and beating them. Yeah, that was thrilling. Made me happy to be a woman again. I came back to the circus renewed. I owe it to you."

"Well, I'm glad I could help."

"I didn't mean to imply that killing two men was, like, a good thing," Jill said. "I'm sorry, I just had never seen anything like that before."

"I get it."

"I told Bill Weatherly all about it," she said. "He's looking forward to meeting you, and shooting against you."

"He is?" Roxy asked. "He doesn't care if a woman beats him?"

"Oh, he doesn't think you're going to beat him," Jill said. "Bill's real . . . full of himself."

16

"What else can you tell me about him?"

"He's handsome, not as young as he used to be, but still very good in the sack."

Roxy wasn't shocked, just surprised. But she didn't show it.

"You've been to bed with him?"

"Oh my, yes," she said. "He's bedded most of the women here—even Lulu Mae."

"Why is it unusual that he's even bedded Lulu Mae?" Roxy asked.

"She's our bearded lady." Jill laughed.

"Is that true?" Roxy asked. "He bedded the bearded lady?"

"Oh yeah."

"Why would he do that?" Roxy asked. "Just to prove he could."

"Probably," Jill said, "but you'll also understand when you see Lulu Mae."

Chapter Five

They drank the coffee and talked about other members of the circus family.

"Some of us have been together since the carnival days," Jill said. "Some just since we became a circus."

"How do you become a circus?" Roxy asked.

Jill laughed. "You add lions, and a ringmaster."

"How many lions do you have?"

"Two."

"Where did you get them?"

"One from Africa, one from a zoo in St. Louis."

"And who owns them?" Roxy asked. "I guess I mean, who owns the circus?"

"I do."

"You do?" Roxy was surprised.

"Does it surprise you that a woman could own a circus?" Jill asked.

"I guess not."

"Well," Jill said, "I own it with a partner. You'll meet him before the competition."

"Is it the sharpshooter, Weatherly?"

"No," Jill said, "Bill just works here."

Other circus members came and went, had coffee, maybe a sandwich—which Roxy turned down.

Then two men and a woman came, all of them over six feet tall.

"What's she doin' here?" one man asked.

"She's my guest."

"You know rubes ain't allowed back here."

"Shes not a rube, Stefan," Jill said. "I told you, she's my guest."

"She's beautiful," the tall woman said. She was blonde and full-bodied, with powerful thighs and forearms.

"Yes, she is," Jill agreed.

"Is she going to work here?" They all had accents, probably German, from Roxy's experience. The men looked to be in their 40's, the woman in her 30's.

"She's competing in the sharpshooting contest," Jill explained.

"She's going to shoot against Bill?" the woman asked.

"She is."

The woman got a cup of coffee, came back to the table and put her hand out to Roxy.

"I am Greta," she said. "Good luck. I hope you beat him."

Roxy shook her hand. "Thanks."

The two men got coffee, gave Roxy a sour look, and walked away. The woman followed them.

"What do they do?" Roxy asked.

"Most of the heavy lifting," Jill said. "And they do a strong man act."

"Strong man?"

"And woman."

"Are they—is she married to one of them?"

"No," Jill said, "they're her brothers."

"Did she sleep with Bill Weatherly?"

19

"Oh yea," Jill said, "but I think only once. Her brothers found out about it and warned him off."

"Ah," Roxy said. "So it causes trouble?"

"What? Bill sleepin' with all the women?" Jill nodded. "Sometimes. If they fall in love with him they usually leave."

"Do you fire them?"

"No," Jill said, "they just leave, because he doesn't love them back."

"I've known men like that."

"You're pretty young," Jill said.

"Still, I've known men like that, who can't love."

"Well," Jill said, "you'll like him, everybody does. Like can't do any harm."

Jill set her cup aside, leaned her elbows on the table.

"I've got a proposition for you," she said.

"What?"

"Come work for me," Jill said.

"Doing what?" Roxy asked.

"What you do best," Jill said. "Shooting."

"How would Bill feel about that?"

"He doesn't do the hiring," Jill said, "I do."

"But he won't like it."

"If you beat him," Jill said, "he'll understand."

"If I beat him do I get the five hundred dollars?"

"Oh yeah," Jill said. "It's a bonus. Every time he wins he gets the money."

"Has anyone ever beaten him?"

"No."

"So how will he feel if I get the money?"

"He'll probably respect you."

"I'm looking for my father," Roxy said. "I heard he might be here."

"Here in the circus?"

"No, here in Blackhawk."

"And if he isn't?"

"I'll move on, keep looking."

"So move on with us," Jill said. "We'll look together."

Roxy thought a moment, then pushed her cup aside and matched Jill's pose, elbows on the table.

"Why don't we wait and see what happens?" she suggested.

"Okay," Jill said. "It was just an offer." She stood up. "Come on, I want you to meet my partner."

Chapter Six

Roxy followed Jill to a wagon that looked like a medicine wagon, the kind that drummers used to try to sell their cure-all. On the wooden sides was painted POMERANTZ CIRCUS.

"Pomerantz?" Roxy asked.

"My partner's name."

"So does he own most of the circus?" Roxy asked.

"No," Jill said. "We're equal partners, but we put his circus together with my carnival, and kept his name."

There was a door in the back of the wagon. Jill stepped up and knocked on it. When a man answered he was tall, longhaired, with an eye patch over his left eye. His craggy face was oddly beautiful, and Roxy could not guess his age.

"Is it time?" he asked.

"Almost," Jill said, "but this is the lady I told you about, Roxy Doyle."

"Ah," he said, "the Lady Gunsmith." He stepped down and closed the door.

"Roxy, this is my partner," Jill said. "Derek Pomerantz."

"I'm pleased to meet you," Roxy said.

They shook hands.

"Jill says you're going to beat Bill Weatherly at his own game."

"I'm going to try," she said. "But there are other competitors."

"Oh yes," Pomerantz said, "but they have no chance, whereas you do."

"You've never seen me shoot."

"We know your reputation."

"Reputations can be exaggerated."

"Is yours?"

"Yes."

"You're not as fast as they say?" he asked.

"Faster."

"Then what's the exaggeration?"

"I haven't killed as many men as they say," Roxy told him.

Pomerantz looked at Jill. "She'll do. Did you make the offer?"

"Sort of."

"What's that mean?"

"We didn't talk money," Jill sad, "beyond the five hundred."

"Ah," Pomerantz said, looking at Roxy. "Are you gonna hold out?"

"I'm just not ready to answer, yet."

"After the contest," Jill told Pomerantz, "we'll talk again."

"You know," Pomerantz said to Roxy, "if Bill beats you, we won't offer you as much."

"That makes sense," Roxy said.

Pomerantz laughed and looked at Jill. "Oh yeah, she'll do."

Jill touched Roxy's arm. "Come on, let's go over to the contest site. You can meet the other competitors."

"I'll be there before you begin," Pomerantz promised. "I'm looking forward to it."

"So am I," Roxy said, and followed Jill.

As they walked away Roxy asked, "What happened to his eye?"

"He tells a different story every time," Jill said. "Once he said he was working with a lady archer and she shot the eye out. Another time he said a lion swiped it out. Still another time he said a jealous husband knocked it out. You see? Different every time."

"How old is he?"

"Nobody knows that, either," Jill said. "Now stop asking questions and concentrate on the contest. You'll meet the other competitors, and then you'll all meet Bill."

Roxy nodded.

She decided that concentrating on the contest was a good idea, because she needed that $500 prize money.

***

The other competitors were all men, all from town or the surrounding county. One owned a gun shop in town, another was a hunter, and still others were ranch hands.

They were all milling about outside of a tent which Jill called the big top. The contest was going to take place indoors. Roxy met the others, but didn't remember all the names. There were too many. When some of them were gone, it would become easier.

"I am Fritz the Ringmaster," a man in a top hat and tuxedo said. He looked to be 50 years old. "The sharpshooting contest will be done in five rounds. The first round will involve shooting at playing cards. The second will be shooting at targets held by our young ladies. And the third round will involve targets that will be tossed into the air. There are twenty four of you. Six will be eliminated after each round. That means when the three rounds are over, there will be six left. We are not going to tell you what you'll be shooting at during the fourth round." He smiled. "That will be a surprise. Only the top two will move on to the fifth and final round."

"Why can't we shoot outdoors?" a man asked.

"There will be spectators seated inside," the ringmaster said. "We've sold a lot of tickets, and they'll want to sit and watch. Any more questions?"

Nobody spoke up.

"All right then," the ringmaster said. "Wait here and I'll come and get you all when it's time. Have your guns ready."

Chapter Seven

The men broke up into groups, talking amongst themselves while they waited. But they all seemed to be trying to keep their eyes off of Roxy. Oh, they wanted to look, but they didn't want her to see them looking. She wondered if word had gotten around town about who she was and why she was there?

She stood off to one side, avoiding them so the men wouldn't have to try to avoid her. Her weapons were ready, having been cleaned the night before.

They heard some noise from inside the tent, the cheering of a crowd, and the loud voice of the ringmaster.

"Was that a lion?" a man asked.

"Yeah, I think they got lions . . . or tigers, or somethin'," somebody else said.

"Geez," a young man said, "tigers?"

At that point the ringmaster stuck his head out of the tent while a calliope started playing inside.

"Okay, file in. Make a straight line. I got everybody's name. When I call you, you'll step forward and take your shots."

"Shots at what?" somebody asked.

"Playing cards," another voice said. "Wasn't you listenin'?"

"Shaddup!" the first man said.

"Shut up, all of you!" the ringmaster snapped. "Don't worry, I'll be telling you what to shoot at. Now come on!"

They got in line with Roxy in the middle, and filed into the tent. She saw all the people on the raised stands, listening to the music and watching some clowns run around. Off to one side there was a cage with two lions in it.

The ringmaster led them to the center of the tent, and when people saw them they started applauding.

As the ringmaster raised his hand, the music stopped, and the clowns ran off,

"Ladies and gentlemen," he called, "it's time for our sharpshooting contest. We have twenty-three men, and one lady, going up against our sharpshooter . . . and here he is, the great Bill Weatherly!"

A man came out, wearing buckskins and a wide-brimmed hat, carrying a rifle. On his hip he wore a pearl handled revolver.

A pretty girl came out with him, wearing a dress that belonged in a saloon. They took a bow together, and then she went and stood thirty or so feet from him.

She was wearing some sort of headdress with feathers sticking up from it. Weatherly drew and fired three times. Each shot took a feather off her head. The crowd loved it and applauded. The ringmaster spoke again while Weatherly reloaded.

"If any of these fine folks can beat Bill," he said, "they'll win five hundred dollars."

That made everyone applaud even louder.

"If Bill wins, well, he gets the money."

The crowd booed.

"Now, we're gonna start with the challengers shooting first, and then Bill will shoot."

The pretty girl brought out a stand with a flat board on it. On the top was a ridge where she was able to wedge playing cards into, facing front.

"All those cards are fives," the ringmaster said. "Fives of hearts, diamonds, spades and clubs. Each competitor must choose a card and shoot out all the symbols. We'll start with Carl Webber. Carl is the town barber."

Webber toed the line, squinted, and fired five times.

"Miss!" the girl shouted when she checked the target.

"How many misses, Laurie?" the ringmaster asked.

"All," she said. "He didn't hit the card at all."

The crowd laughed.

The ringmaster looked at Webber and asked loudly. "Which suit did you aim for?"

"The spades," the man said.

Laurie checked the cards again.

"Nope. He didn't hit any of the cards!" she called out.

Webber looked embarrassed.

"I'm sorry," the ringmaster said, loudly. "You're elimi-nated."

Webber walked off.

"Next is Carl Cantrell. Carl is the town . . ."

Roxy didn't listen to the names of the competitors, or their jobs. It wasn't important that she remember them. Maybe when they got down to the last five or six it would be different.

Cantrell fired at the five of hearts, and hit one. His other four shots missed completely. Roxy wondered what these people were doing there?

"Eliminated!"

The next four men toed the line and fired, and after each one was done the ringmaster shouted, "Eliminated."

He leaned in to the remaining competitors and said, "One of you rubes better hit something!"

That was the second time Roxy had heard the word "rubes." She'd have to ask Jill what it meant.

The next man stepped to the line. He was tall, dressed in a dark suit, looked more like a gambler than a marksman. Roxy hadn't heard his name.

He fired five times. Laurie stepped to the cards.

"What did you choose?" the ringmaster asked.

"Diamonds."

"He chose the five of diamonds, Laurie," the ringmaster called. "How did he do?"

"Five hits!" she called back.

"Well," the ringmaster said, loudly. "That was fine shooting." Then, in a voice only the competitors could hear, he said, "Now maybe we're getting somewhere."

Chapter Eight

The competition continued, and Roxy started to realize that she was going to go last. Maybe Jill had planned it that way. So as she watched 8 of the others managed to hit their targets.

"This is awful," the ringmaster said, so only she and the others could hear. "We only wanted to eliminate six at the time. Now we're already down to nine."

"The lady still has to shoot," the tall man in the dark suit said.

"Yeah, right," the ringmaster said. He returned to his position and said, "The last competitor is . . . Roxy Doyle."

Roxy stepped to the line, drew and fired before anyone could say or do anything. Then she holstered her pistol and waited.

"Which card?" the ringmaster asked.

"Hearts," she said.

Laurie stepped to the cards.

"Five clean hits, right through the hearts."

The crowd was silent, then somebody began to applaud, then more, and eventually everyone joined in.

"Ladies and gentlemen, now Bill Weatherly will shoot."

Weatherly stepped to the line, drew his gun and fired, slightly slower and more deliberate than Roxy had.

"I fired at the five of spades," he announced.

"Five direct hits!" Laurie called, and the crowd applauded. Weatherly took a bow.

"Ladies and gents, we'll resume with the contest in a half an hour. Meanwhile, enjoy the show!"

The ringmaster walked off, waving at the competitors to follow him. They went back outside, where they had first assembled.

"Okay," he said, "some of you can shoot, so let's see if we can salvage something from this. We intended to take at least eighteen of you to the second round, but we have ten."

"What's the second round?" the tall man asked.

"You'll be using your rifles."

"So eliminate half," the man suggested. "Then we can go to the third round with five of us and Weatherly, and you can eliminate three."

"That sounds good to me," Roxy said. "That'll put us in the last round with Weatherly and two of us."

"You won't be there, girlie," said another man, a ranch hand from a local spread. "It'll be two of us men."

"Don't be so sure," the tall man said. "You saw her shoot."

"Yeah, yeah," the man said, "she got lucky."

Before anyone could say anything else Bill Weatherly stepped from the tent to join them.

"Nice shooting, folks," he said. He was speaking to everyone, but looking at Roxy. She looked back. She could see why the women in the circus would sleep with him. He was tall, broad shouldered, and handsome.

"I just wanted to wish you all good luck in round two."

"We don't have as many as we'd planned, Bill, so here's what we're gonna do . . ."

The ringmaster put his arm around Weatherly's shoulder and they went back into the tent.

The tall man came over to Roxy and stood in front of her. He had an angular face with a pointed jaw and piercing blue eyes.

"You shot very well," he said.

"So did you."

"These others are going to fall by the wayside, you know," he said.

"I know."

"It'll be you, me and Weatherly."

"I know that, too. Why are you dressed like a gambler?" she asked.

"Because I am a gambler," he said. "My name's John Steel. I need this five hundred as a stake."

"Well," she said, "I'm sorry."

He smiled.

"We'll see who's sorry," he said. "I wish you luck, though."

"You, too."

As he turned and walked away she saw Jill and Pomerantz coming toward her.

"That was impressive," Pomerantz said.

"Thanks, but it's not over," she said.

"Well, it'll be interesting," he said. "Have you seen Weatherly?"

"He just went inside with the ringmaster."

"I'll catch him inside."

As Pomerantz went into the tent Jill smiled and said, "You're making me look good."

"I'm glad."

In a surprise move Jill hugged Roxy, kissed her on the cheek gently and said, "Keep it up and I'll make my offer more appealing."

The woman gave her an extra squeeze before going into the tent which made Roxy wonder just what she meant by that.

Chapter Nine

"Ladies and gentlemen," Fritz called out, "we have volunteers."

He waved and they came out, five young women who worked for the circus, in one job or another.

"They do many different jobs around here," he told the crowd, "but tonight they have volunteered to hold targets in their hands."

The crowd applauded. Some of the girls bowed, and others laughed.

"We have enough confidence in the ten remaining contestants that they won't shoot one of our girls."

The crowd laughed.

"Each girl will hold targets for two shooters. I will assign each girl to their shooter. First, Mary will hold targets for John Steel and local boy, Dan Tilson."

Tilson was the ranch hand who laughed at the idea of Roxy winning the contest.

"The targets are clay," the ringmaster explained. "All the shooter has to do is hit them, shatter them. Doesn't matter if the hit is dead center. But if it's close to a tie, though, then the size of the remaining piece will decide. The shooter who leaves the smallest piece in the girl's hand moves on."

He gave Mary two clay plates, which she held over her head, one in each hand. She was two hundred feet from the men with the rifles.

Steel and Tilson were to aim and fire together. They shouldered their rifles and fired a second apart. Steel's plates shattered completely. Tilson's plate broke, but left half of it in the girl's hand.

"Steel wins and moves on," Fritz called out.

The crowd applauded, as much for the girl as for the winner.

"The next girl is Laurie. She'll hold targets for . . ."

Roxy still wasn't paying attention to names, except for Steel, and Weatherly. She was convinced that the three of them would be in the final round.

By the time the ringmaster called her name, four men had moved on. She was paired with a man named Aarons. The girl holding their plates was Diane.

Roxy raised her rifle, pointed, did not aim, and shattered her plate completely. To her surprise, Aarons did the same.

"A tie," the ringmaster announced. "They'll shoot again. Diane, move back a hundred feet."

A clown helped her find the proper distance.

"Shoot!" the ringmaster called out.

Roxy raised her rifle and fired, shattering her plate. Aarons aimed, took his time, and fired. He hit the plate and it shattered, but Diane jerked her hands down and grabbed it.

The ringmaster ran to the girl and examined her hand, then waved at the clown to come over and get her. The figure with the orange hair and red nose led her away.

The ringmaster came back to where Roxy and Aarons were standing.

"Mr. Aarons shattered his plate, but he nicked the girl's hand. Doyle wins and moves on."

There was applause.

"Ladies and Gentlemen, now Bill Weatherly will shoot.

A girl named Billie held up two plates and Weatherly, shot, shattering both.

The crowd applauded.

"Ladies and gents, we will resume in half an hour," Fritz said. "Until then, enjoy the show."

They filed out of the tent and Aarons stormed away, fuming and complaining that "the girl moved!"

Roxy went up to the ringmaster.

"How's her hand?"

"Just a nick," he said. "I don't even think it was a bullet, just a shard of the clay plate."

"Too bad," Roxy said.

"Hey," Fritz said, "she volunteered."

"Still . . ."

The ringmaster walked back into the tent.

Roxy turned, looked at Steel and the other three men.

"How's the girl?" the gambler asked.

"She'll live."

"I wonder if the remaining four will still volunteer?" a man named Baker said.

"I guess we'll see," said a man called Proctor.

"There won't be any girls," Roxy said.

The four men looked at her.

"How do you know?" Baker asked.

"She listens," Steel said.

"What's that mean?" Proctor asked.

"The ringmaster said the third round will be targets that are tossed into the air," Roxy said.

"That's right," the fifth man a youngster named Freddie Brown said.

"You haven't spoken all day," Baker said to Freddie.

"That's because I let my shooting talk for me," Freddie said.

"Attaboy!" Steel said, smiling.

Roxy liked him.

Chapter Ten

The competitors lined up outside the tent, waiting to be called in for the third round. Once again, Jill came out to see Roxy.

"You're doin' wonderfully," she said.

"Thanks. Too bad about the girl getting hurt."

"She'll be fine," Jill said. "Circus people are a hearty stock. You just keep shooting the way you're shooting."

"It's the only way I know how."

"You've got these men worried."

"Really?" Roxy asked. "Mr. Steel doesn't look worried at all."

"That's true," Jill said, "but you're a better shot than he is."

"We'll see."

"No, no," Jill said, "you know it already. You know this competition will come down to you and Bill."

Roxy didn't comment.

Jill put her hand on Roxy's shoulder and said, "I'll see you after," and went back inside.

"You have an in with the boss?"

She turned and saw Steel standing there.

"Not really," she said. "We just met yesterday."

"Seems she may be rooting for a woman to win this thing," Steel said.

"Well," Roxy said, "I do need the five hundred dollars."

"I'm sure you do."

"We all do," Baker said, after eavesdropping.

Both Steel and Roxy looked at him, but didn't say anything.

"You two wouldn't be plannin' somethin', would you?" Baker asked.

"Like what?" Steel asked.

"Like maybe workin' together to get rid of the rest of us?" Proctor asked, stepping up.

"They can't get rid of us," Freddie said. "We can only do that ourselves, by missin'."

"Listen to the smart boy," Baker said.

"Nobody asked you, boy," Proctor said. He and Baker were both in their forties. Neither of them wanted to get beat by a kid, a gambler, or a girl.

Fritz came out and said, "Get set."

"What are you gonna be tossin' into the air?" Baker asked.

"You'll see. Now line up."

They did.

***

"Ladies and gentlemen, our final five competitors."

The five of them filed in, Roxy coming in right after John Steel.

"We have glass balls that have been blown just for this kind of competition," Fritz announced. "I personally saw

39

Hugh Cardiff once shoot these balls—hundreds of them. They fly straight and true because they're round."

"Jesus," Baker said. "There's gonna be glass all over the place."

"Only if you hit any of them," Freddie said.

"Shut up, kid!" Proctor said.

Roxy and Steel laughed.

"First to shoot will be Del Baker. Six balls will be tossed into the air. He will get six shots."

Baker stepped forward. Roxy was surprised to see the girl with the injured hand holding the balls.

"Throw!"

She tossed the balls into the air one after the other, timed perfectly. The big top was high enough for the balls to sail above everyone with no problems.

Baker fired six shots.

"Two hits, four misses," Fritz called.

"Shit!" Baker cursed. "She threw them crooked."

"You just can't hit a moving target, Baker," Freddie said, laughing.

"Oh yeah? Let's see how good you are, sonny."

"Next will be Freddie Brown!" the ringmaster called.

The same girl tossed the balls, so there would be no controversy about it. Same girl tossing the balls in the same way.

Freddie fired six times.

"Four hit, two misses."

Only the top three would advance. Nobody was eliminated until four people had fired.

"Next is Lem Proctor."

Proctor stepped up, fired six times. The balls shattered audibly. There was no question of how many hits and misses.

"Three hits, three misses," Fritz said. "Next, John Steel."

Roxy watched him intently. The girl threw, he fired. She watched him, but heard the balls shatter.

"Six hit!" Fritz called. "Baker is eliminated."

"Shit!" Baker swore, and stormed off.

Steel came back and stood by Roxy.

"Nice shooting," she said.

"Thanks," he said. "The kid's not bad, either."

"No," she said, "in a few years he might be unbeatable."

"But not now?"

"No," she said, "not now."

She stepped to the line and waited for a girl to throw the balls into the air. She drew and fired. Each glass ball exploded, disintegrated, with nothing left to fall to the ground.

"Six hits!" Fritz called out. "Proctor is eliminated. That leaves Steel, Doyle, and Freddie. Bill Weatherly will now shoot."

Weatherly appeared from the other side of the tent, took his position, and fired six measured shots.

"Six hits!" Fritz shouted. "Freddie Brown is eliminated. The last round will be Jim Steel, Roxy Doyle, and Bill Weatherly. We'll start in one hour!"

Chapter Eleven

"Are all the people going to stay?" Roxy asked.

"They've been here this long," John Steel said. "Why not?"

They sat across from each other at a table, eating. They were being fed before the last round of the competition started. Bill Weatherly wasn't eating with them.

Jill came walking over with a plate and sat down next to Steel, across from Roxy.

"You two are special," she said, "but do you think you can beat Bill?"

"I have to," Steel said. "I need the stake."

Jill looked at Roxy. "You."

"I can beat him."

"Pomerantz wants me to ask you not to beat Bill."

"What?"

"What's this about?" Steel asked.

"He's not worried about you."

"He doesn't think I can beat him?"

"He doesn't care if you beat him," she said. "You're a man."

"Ah . . ."

Jill looked at Roxy. "What do you say?"

"Tell your partner I'm going to beat Weatherly," Roxy said. "There's nothing else I can do."

Jill smiled. "Attagirl! That's what I told him."

"And you don't mind?" Roxy asked.

"I don't mind at all," Jill said. "As a matter of fact, I wouldn't mind seeing Bill taken down a peg or two."

"And getting beat by a woman would do that to him?" Steel asked.

"Yes," Jill said.

"And how would he react if I beat him?"

"He wouldn't like it," Jill said, "but he'd take it in stride." Roxy thought she saw Jill rub her shoulder up against Steel's. She found herself wondering if something was going on there.

Jill stood up and took her half-finished plate.

"I'll go tell Derek what you said," she told Roxy, and walked away.

"She's gonna be very happy if you beat Weatherly," Steel said.

"Looks that way."

"Did this contest bring you to town?" Steel asked.

"No," Roxy said. "I didn't even know the circus was here until I rode in. What about you?"

"Oh yeah," he said, "I was in a town nearby and heard about the five hundred. I rode right over."

Roxy felt bad for the man, but she thought she needed the money more than he did. She had to find her father, and Steel just wanted the money to play cards.

"Well," she said, "I guess the best shot will win."

"I guess so," Steel said, with a smile that made her heart flutter a little bit. She wondered how often the man used that smile in a card game? He was charming, and she was going to have to get away from him if she wanted to beat him.

"Excuse me," she said, standing. "I need some time to myself before we go back in."

"Sure," he said, "I understand that. Gotta get ready."

She nodded, said, "See you inside," and walked away.

***

Jill went into the big top and found Derek Pomerantz standing off to one side.

"Any luck?" he asked.

"No."

"Did you try hard?"

"I tried my best, Derek," she said. "She's determined to win."

"If she does," Pomerantz said, "it'll break Bill. You know that."

"Actually, I don't," she said. "I have more faith in Bill's ego than you do."

"Well, I'm more concerned about his ability to put this behind him and continue performing as we move on."

"Why are you so convinced she's going to beat him," Jill asked.

"You've seen her shoot," he replied. "It's uncanny. She's a natural."

"Well," Jill said, "I guess that's why they call her Lady Gunsmith."

"And you knew who she was when you first signed her up?" he asked.

"Oh, yeah."

"And you still signed her."

"I want her to work for us, Derek," Jill said.

"And you think you can get her to do that?"

"I think I can, yes."

"And what are your motives?"

"Why, to make us better, what else?"

"Are you sure you don't have a more . . . personal interest in this young woman?"

"Come on, Derek," Jill said. "I'm a professional."

Chapter Twelve

Originally, Roxy was only concerned with the $500 prize money, and how it would help her in her search for her father. But suddenly other people's feelings and needs were involved. John Steel needed the money in order to continue gambling. Derek Pomerantz needed her to lose so his sharp-shooter, Bill Weatherly, wouldn't lose face. And Jill—well, the older woman had her own reasons for wanting Roxy to win.

But Roxy couldn't concern herself with all the feelings and needs and egos involved. All she could—and should—be worried about were her own needs.

So she walked around, got her mind settled, her focus, and then walked back to the big tent to finish what she had started.

Fritz the ringmaster called them back in.

Roxy and John Steel entered the tent together, and the crowd began to applaud. Across from them stood Bill Weatherly, waving at the roaring crowd and looking totally unconcerned.

"Ladies and gentlemen," Fritz announced, "these three shooters are so closely matched that we will have to do something special to separate them. Once again we'll be using the glass balls, but we're going to need a variety of our girls to toss them, because we're going to do a best of one hundred."

The crowd gasped, many people wondering if they would be there into the night.

"We're going to separate the finalists so they'll be able to shoot at the same time. The only pause in the action will be to change girls because one girl will not be able to toss a hundred of these balls into the air. We're afraid their arms would fall off!"

The crowd laughed at that.

"We will also pause for each shooter to reload their rifles. Their pistols will remain in their holsters, this time around."

The crowd oohed.

"So, Ladies, come and get your shooter and take them to their mark."

Three girls came forward, each taking the hand of a shooter and walked them to their spots. They were placed far enough apart that the flight of their glass balls would not intersect, and there'd be no confusion.

"We also have someone keeping count in each case," Fritz went on. "Our wonderful clowns will be doing that."

Three clowns came into the tent and took up a position near the shooters.

"And yes, ladies and gentlemen," Fritz said, "clowns can count."

That brought more laughter.

"All right," Fritz said. "Ladies, are you ready?"

The three girls nodded and waved, indicating their readiness. They each had large sacks next to them on the ground.

"Marksmen—and lady—are you ready""

Roxy, Steel and Weatherly waved."

"Audience, are you ready?" Fritz asked.

The crowd replied with an enthusiastic "Yes!"

"Very well. Ladies," Fritz said, "whenever you're ready, reach into the bag and start tossing your targets into the air. But wait!"

The girls had started to reach into their bag, but now stopped.

"We have something else for each of you," Fritz told the girls.

Three more clowns came into the tent and ran to the girls, handing each of them a parasol.

"That's so you don't get shattered glass in your hair or eyes."

The girls accepted the parasols, while the audience laughed.

"All right," Fritz called out, "start tossing."

The girls reached into the bags and started throwing balls into the air, which the shooters then shattered with a bullet. One girl tossed them in a very measured fashion, while another seemed to be throwing them as fast as she could. The third girl—Roxy's—didn't seem to be able to get into a rhythm until she decided to put the parasol down.

For that reason, it was difficult for Roxy to get her rhythm. Yet in spite of that, she still hadn't missed any of the balls.

Steel had the girl who was tossing the balls as fast as she could. He was firing just as quickly, and not missing.

Bill Weatherly's girl was being very measured as she flipped balls into the air, and he was matching her. Roxy had a feeling they might have worked things out before they started. They seemed to be operating together like a well-oiled machine. She also wondered if the girl had received instructions from either Jill or her partner, Pomerantz, in order to give Weatherly an advantage.

Roxy was busy with her targets, and didn't know if her two opponents had missed any, at all.

Chapter Thirteen

After 75 targets were thrown and counted they took a break so the girls could decide amongst themselves who was next to do the tossing.

Roxy and Steel attended to their rifles, to make sure they'd continue to function. Bill Weatherly walked off, left the tent, and would return when it was time to continue.

None of the appreciative crowd had left. After spending so much of the day watching, they were anxious to see who the winner was going to be.

The clowns gathered in a corner of the tent, waiting to start again.

One of the clowns—who was not among those counting—was very interested in the proceedings. He was specifically watching Roxy while she fired at her targets.

"Can't keep your eyes off of her, can you?" Jill asked, coming up behind him.

"Huh? No, uh, I'm just interested, like everybody else, in who's gonna win."

"Lester," Jill said, "you've been watching her like a hawk all day. What's up?"

"Nothin'," Lester the Clown said. He had tufts of blue hair on his head. Big black circles around his eyes and very red lips, all on white face paint.

"Well, we don't need you here, and there's other work to do. I'll tell you who won."

"Yeah," Lester said, "sure . . ."

"Lester," she said, as he started away.

"Huh?"

"You're still on probation, you know," Jill said. "Don't let me catch you standing around doing nothing again."

"Yes, Ma'am."

He hurried away.

***

Lester's real name was Les Collier. He had only been hired as a clown several weeks earlier, when he ran into the circus as it was traveling. He was afoot, his horse having stepped in a chuckhole and broken his leg. He was carrying his saddle, staggering down the road, when he heard the wagons approaching from behind. He dropped the saddle, turned and waved. They stopped and picked him up.

By the time they reached Blackhawk, Collier had decided to stay with them a while, if they would have him. He asked to be trained as a clown, and they agreed—especially once he said he didn't need to be paid.

In reality, Collier was wanted in several states for robbery, and in one state for murder. He had been on the run when his horse broke down. Once he was with the circus, he thought it would be a good place to hide out. So he asked to be a clown, which enabled him to hide behind the make-up.

Hiding and on the run, Collier—or "Lester the Clown"—was suspicious of people who came to the circus as something other than a spectator. So he kept an eye on Roxy—

which wasn't hard—and found out that her name was Roxy "Doyle."

He had to find out if she was related to another Doyle he knew of.

***

"What's the score?"

Fritz the Ringmaster turned and looked at Jill.

"Wouldn't you like to know?"

"I would," she said, "since I'm the boss."

"Well," Fritz said, "you'll find out at the same time everyone else does."

"Fritz—"

"I'm in charge as long as there are people in the big top," he told her. "Unless you want to fire me now?"

"I don't want to fire you, Fritz," she said, then added, "now."

"Then let me get on with my job."

"By all means."

She walked away. There was no one else who knew the exact count of targets. Each shooter's clown and girl knew their total, but no one knew all three except Fritz.

As she walked away Pomerantz appeared in her path.

"Problem?" he asked.

"I was just wondering about the totals," she said.

"And?"

"Fritz won't tell me."

"Well," Pomerantz said, "we know how territorial Fritz is. He'll tell us when it's all over."

"Yes, he will," she said. "Excuse me."

As she walked past him he said, "Jill?"

She turned.

"Will I see you tonight?"

"Not tonight, Derek," she said. "I—I'm going to be busy."

"I see."

She touched his face and said, "I have work to do."

He watched her walk away, wondering how much of her work had to do with Bill Weatherly?

Chapter Fourteen

The competition resumed.

The girls were each hoping there were only 25 targets left to toss into the air. Although they were alternating, they were still getting very tired.

As the shooting commenced Fritz looked down at the slip of paper he was holding. He'd collected the scores from each of the three counting clowns, and was both pleased and worried. Pleased that the competition might be going on a little longer, but worried about the girls.

Each shooter, at this point, has shattered all 75 of the glass balls they'd fired at. Not one miss. If it ended in a 100-100-100 tie, they'd have to go on.

Maybe they should draft some of the clowns into service to toss the targets.

***

Roxy and Steel had spoken during the break. Bill Weatherly, as usual, stood off to the other side of the tent, away from them.

"Miss any?" Steel asked Roxy.

She debated answering the question truthfully, or lying. She decided on the truth.

"No," she said.

"Not one?"

"Not one. You?"

He hesitated. "No, me, neither."

She wondered if he was answering truthfully? She decided that he was. He seemed like the type, even though she was sure he had run plenty of bluffs at the poker table. This was different.

"I wonder about Weatherly," he said.

"Given what it says on the posters," Roxy said, "I would say he should never miss—ever!"

"It only takes one," Steel said, "to make one of us five hundred dollars richer."

"I'm not going to miss, Mr. Steel."

"Just call me John, or Johnny," he said.

"All right," she said, smiling. "I don't intend to miss . . . Johnny."

***

When the shooting started again, Roxy kept her mind on her task. She put Johnny Steel's charming smile, Jill's motives, and Derek Pomerantz's pleas for her to lose, in the back of her mind. At this point in the competition, there was no room for distractions.

She also hadn't been counting, so she had no idea when they were getting to the end. So when Fritz called a halt to the proceedings, she was both surprised and relieved. Her arms were starting to ache, and her rifle barrel seemed red hot.

"Ladies and gentlemen," Fritz called out, "each of our competitors has fired at ninety-nine targets. Let's give them a round of applause."

The crowd agreed and clapped their hands for a long time.

"Now, to the business at hand," Fritz yelled. "All three of the shooters . . . have hit every target. All ninety-nine!"

More applause.

"So this last one is very important. I thought we'd let them each go separately, so we could really watch all three. What do you say to that?"

Roxy had to admit that this man knew how to play to the crowd. He was getting them all riled up.

"Very well," Fritz said. "Mr. Steel will fire at his final target first." Then he held up his finger. "That is, his final target unless we end in a tie."

Steel stepped forward. For this final target the girls had been replaced by male clowns. Fritz thought that a man would be able to toss the glass ball higher.

Roxy wondered how many holes were in the top of the tent, and how they intended to fix them, or replace it? She wondered if anyone had thought about the three hundred holes when they decided to hold the contest inside?

Steel's clown threw the ball as hard as he could. The gambler raised his rifle, fired . . . and shattered the ball.

"One hundred out of one hundred!" Fritz shouted, and the crowd roared.

Steel played it up also, waving to the stands as he took his place next to Roxy.

"Nice," she said.

"Thanks."

"Now Roxy Doyle!" Fritz shouted.

Roxy stepped up and waited for her clown to throw the ball. As it sailed up toward the top of the tent she fired and shattered it as it was still rising.

"One hundred out of one hundred!" Fritz yelled.

The crowd was enthused.

"And now our own Bill Weatherly will shoot at his final target!" Fritz called.

Weatherly stepped to his spot at the other end of the tent. His clown grabbed a ball and heaved it in the air. Roxy noticed that there wasn't much of an arc. The man seemed to have thrown it across the tent, rather than at the roof.

Weatherly tracked the ball with his rifle barrel and fired. It shattered above the crowd, which gasped, then applauded.

Roxy wondered if that had been planned?

"One hundred out of one hundred! Don't go anywhere, folks. We have a three way tie!"

Chapter Fifteen

"This has never happened before," Jill told the three of them.

She had lined them up, feeling the need to address them all.

"Are we going to split the money?" Steel asked. A third wouldn't be much of a stake, but it would be something.

"Is that what you want to do?" Pomerantz asked. "Any of you?"

"Not me," Bill Weatherly said, with a smile. "I want the whole caboodle."

"So do I," Roxy said.

"And me," Steel agreed.

"Then what do we do?" Jill asked.

"We keep shootin'," Bill Weatherly said. "I'll bet these two feel the same." He looked at Roxy and Steel and spoke to them for the first time that day. "You're both hellishly good marksmen—and women. Sorry."

"No problem," Roxy said.

"Then," Pomerantz said, "the next question is, what do you shoot at? More glass balls?"

"We'll run out," Jill said.

"Cards," Pomerantz said.

"We did that," Jill said. "We need something else, something new."

"I have a suggestion," John Steel said.

They all looked at him.

"Poker chips." He made a circle with the forefinger and thumb of his left hand, and then poked his right forefingers through it. "You have to hit it dead center, put a hole in it. If you just chip it, or you miss, you lose."

"You've shot at poker chips before, haven't you?" Weatherly asked, with a grin. "You're a gambler, right?"

"I am a gambler," Steel admitted, "and I have done it before, but that doesn't make it easier."

"Poker chips," Pomerantz said, looking at Jill.

"It could work," Jill said.

"What about you two?" Pomerantz asked. "What do you think of Steel's idea?"

"I think it's sneaky as hell," Weatherly said, still grinning, "but I'm game." He looked at Roxy. "How about you, Miss Doyle?"

"Just call me Roxy."

"Okay, Roxy," Weatherly said. "What do you say?"

"I say let's shoot."

***

Jill and Pomerantz went into the big top to explain their decision to Fritz. The ringmaster went along with it whole-heartedly, because it would keep him in front of the crowd.

He made the announcement, explaining that the three competitors would now be shooting at poker chips that would be lodged into the board where the playing cards had recently stood.

"They must put a hole through the center of the chip," Fritz went on. "If they simply nick it, or miss it completely—one chip—they'll be eliminated."

The crowd seemed excited by what was coming.

Fritz turned to the competitors.

"Are you ready?"

All three waved their right hands.

A board was brought out—bullet holes in it from past competitions—and three poker chips were lodged into the top of it. One was blue, one was red, and one was white. Roxy thought that was a nice touch. Maybe they should even have assigned a different value to each color, but she could suggest that later if there was still a tie.

"This time," Fritz called out, "we're going to let Bill Weatherly shoot first."

Weatherly stepped up to his mark, aimed his rifle, and fired three times. He then backed off, cradled the rifle, and waited calmly.

A clown ran up to the board, examined the three chips, then turned and waved to Fritz.

"Three direct hits!" Fritz announced.

The crowd cheered and applauded.

"Next, Roxy Doyle."

Roxy toed her line, raised her rifle and fired three shots in quick succession. She did what Clint Adams, the Gunsmith, had trained her to do. She did not aim the rifle, but simply pointed it like it was an extension of her finger. That way, he told her, you'll always hit what you point at.

She cradled her rifle and waited.

A clown ran up, took a look, then turned and waved to Fritz.

"Three direct hits!" Fritz called. "That leaves only John Steel to shoot."

The gambler moved up to his line, looked out at his targets, took a deep breath, raised the rifle, aimed and fired three shots.

Chapter Sixteen

"By virtue of a small nick in the third chip—the white one—John Steel has been eliminated!" the ringmaster shouted. "That leaves Roxy Doyle, and our champion sharp-shooter, Bill Weatherly!"

Applause.

Roxy looked over at Steel, who did not seem dejected, at all.

"You did great," she told him.

He smiled that charming smile at her. Not a handsome man, but charming.

"When you're a gambler, you have to learn how to win and how to lose. I wish you good luck, Roxy."

"Are you going to stay and watch?" she asked.

"I sure am," Steel said. "Consider me an enthusiastic spectator."

"Shooters to your marks!" Fritz called.

Roxy turned to wave at Fritz, and when she turned back, Steel was gone. She walked to her mark.

"Ladies and gentlemen," Fritz announced, "the targets will be moved ten feet further away, and will continue to be moved until one of the shooters misses. This is for the five hundred dollar prize!"

"Good luck," Bill Weatherly said to Roxy.

"You, too," she returned. His smile was more handsome than Steel's, just not as charming.

They started to fire . . .

***

Derek Pomerantz watched, hoping that he looked calmer than he felt. It wouldn't be good for business to have their sharpshooter beaten by a girl, but that didn't seem to occur to Jill. She just wanted the girl to come out on top, and then hire on. She wasn't thinking about what that would mean to Bill Weatherly.

She was a selfish bitch.

***

Jill watched the proceeding with her arms crossed over her full breasts. She loved watching the way Roxy Doyle moved. It was economic, every move with meaning. This young woman thought she was already somebody—Lady Gunsmith—but Jill could see that she was meant for bigger things.

This was just the beginning for them . . .

***

Lester the Clown watched as Roxy Doyle competed against Bill Weatherly. He had thought about getting himself involved in the target tossing that had gone on earlier, in the hopes that he could cause Doyle to miss, but it hadn't happened. He was on probation, so they hadn't gotten him involved in the "big show."

He still hadn't determined if she was related to Gavin Doyle. The famed bounty hunter was the stuff of legends and rumors. One rumor had him long dead, but another, more recent rumor had him on the trail of Les Collier.

What if that was not only true, but he had his daughter also looking for Les? Was it coincidence that she was here, competing at the same circus where he was hiding?

Lester the Clown knew he had his own ability with a gun, and thought perhaps he was going to have to put it to good use.

***

Roxy and Weatherly were each putting holes right in the center of their chips. The targets had been moved back three times, already. Roxy wondered what they would do when they ran out of tent? It was already dark outside, too dark to shoot.

Finally, both Jill and Derek Pomerantz came over to confer with Fritz, while Roxy and Weatherly stood off to the side, cradling their hot weapons.

"Maybe we should just shoot at each other and get it over with," Bill Weatherly said, with a smile.

Roxy looked at him. "Have you ever shot another person, Bill? Man or woman?"

"Well, no—"

"If you had," Roxy said, "you'd know it's nothing to joke about."

"You're right," Weatherly said. "I'm sorry. For a moment I forgot who you are."

She didn't react.

"How many men have you killed, Roxy?" he asked. "And at such a young age?"

She looked at him.

"How old are you?" she asked.

"Thirty-five."

"By now you should have faced a man with a gun," she said.

"You're probably right," Weatherly said, "but I'm satisfied shooting my guns at targets."

"Until somebody beats you," she said.

"Somebody's going to beat me, eventually," he said. "Just as somebody will beat you. The only difference is, I won't die."

Now she gave him a hard look, but he turned and looked straight ahead.

Chapter Seventeen

"It's got to come down to the smallest margin," Pomerantz said to Jill and Fritz. "We have to end this so people can go home. Or at least go outside and spend some more money before they leave."

"One chip each," Jill said. "The one who puts their hole more in the center wins."

"Who judges?" Fritz asked.

"We all do," Jill said. "The three of us."

"The smallest, tiniest margin is going to be the difference," Pomerantz said, again.

"All right," Fritz said. "I'll explain it to the crowd, and to the shooters."

"Good," Pomerantz said. "Let's get this damn thing over, already!"

Jill and Pomerantz walked off. Fritz took up his position in the center of the ring and explained the situation to the crowd, and the shooters.

"This will be the last shot," he said, firmly. "It will decide everything."

Each shooter was allowed to choose their own color. Steel chose blue, Roxy red. One chip each was set up on the target board.

"You will fire together," Fritz said, "and then stand back while we examine the chips."

Roxy wondered if it felt odd to John Steel to not be involved, when shooting at poker chips had been his idea?

"Toe your marks!" Fritz called.

They stepped up.

"Fire whenever you're ready!"

Roxy raised her rifle, pointed it and fired.

Bill Weatherly shouldered his rifle, sighted down the barrel, hesitated, then fired.

They both stood back, as instructed, and waited while the ringmaster and the two circus owners stepped up to the board . . .

***

Jill removed the red chip from the board, while Pomerantz removed the blue.

"Well," Pomerantz said, "it's obvious to me that Bill wins."

"You're crazy," Jill said. "Look at this hole. Dead center. Roxy Doyle wins."

"You don't know what you're doing—" Pomerantz started.

"You're just too biased toward Bill—" Jill began.

"Hold it!" Fritz snapped. "Let me have the chips."

Both owners handed over their chips.

Fritz laid one chip over the other, peered through, then reversed them and peered through.

"Okay," he said, "I'll announce the winner."

"Who is it?" Jill asked.

"Who won?" Pomerantz asked.

"You'll find out when I announce it," Fritz said. "Do you have the prize money?"

"Right here," Pomerantz said, patting the breast pocket of his jacket.

"All right," the ringmaster said, "get ready to present it."

Jill and Pomerantz walked away, grousing at each other.

Fritz moved back to his place in the center of the ring.

"Ladies and gentlemen," he called out, "we have a winner!"

Roxy and Bill Weatherly continued to stare straight ahead.

"By the smallest of margins," Fritz announced, "the winner of the five hundred dollar prize is . . . Roxy Doyle!"

The crowd exploded into applause and cheers.

Bill Weatherly turned and offered Roxy his hand. "Congratulations."

"Thank you," she said, shaking his hand.

The handshake done, he turned and walked away. He joined Fritz in the center of the ring and doffed his hat to the crowd.

Fritz waited until the applause died down and then asked, "Miss Doyle, will you join me here, please?"

Roxy moved to the center of the ring to stand with Fritz and Bill Weatherly.

"It was so close," Fritz said, "but by holding the chips one on top of the other, you can see that your shot was more in the center by a hair."

Fritz held the chips that way, and raised them so Roxy could gaze through. With Weatherly's blue chip on top of her red one she was able to see just a sliver of red, that showed her shot was more centered.

She didn't know what to say so as the crowd began to applaud once again, she took off her hat. She'd had her red tresses tucked up under the hat so they wouldn't get in the way, and now they tumbled down to her shoulders.

"And now the prize money!" Fritz said.

Both Jill and Pomerantz headed for the center ring, to stand with the others.

"And presenting the five hundred dollar prize money to Roxy Doyle are the circus co-owners, Derek Pomerantz and Jill Weatherly!"

As Derek Pomerantz presented Roxy with the winner's prize of five hundred dollars, Roxy leaned over to Jill. "Bill Weatherly is your husband?"

Jill smiled at her. "Didn't I mention that?"

Chapter Eighteen

Later, after the crowd had filed out, Roxy sat at a table with Jill having coffee and said, "All you told me was that you slept with him. That lots of the women here at the circus have slept with him."

"That's all true," Jill said. "The women can't resist Bill, and he can't resist the lure of women—any woman!"

"And that doesn't bother you?"

"Not in the least," she said. "If you want to sleep with him, go ahead."

"I don't want to sleep with him."

"Do you prefer to have sex with women?" Jill asked. "Because we could come to some arrangement."

"No," Roxy said, "I like men—"

"So you're more attracted to Johnny Steel, then, and that charming smile of his."

"Why are we talking about this?" Roxy asked. "I'm just wondering why you wanted me to beat your husband."

"Hey, my wanting you to beat him is just business," Jill said. "It doesn't matter that he's my husband. And now that you have beat him, I want you to come work with us."

"I don't know . . ."

"We're heading for Denver, next," she said. "We can have another sharpshooting contest there. Another five hundred dollars. Does that interest you?"

Actually, it did, but it also depended on whether or not she found her father there in Blackhawk.

"When are you leaving for Denver?" she asked.

"Not for three days," Jill said. "We have to finish our days out, here."

"What would you want me to do?"

"Just shoot," Jill said. "You can obviously do trick shooting."

"And what about your husband?" Roxy asked. "What's he going to be doing?"

"The same thing," Jill said. "Why can't we have two trick shooters on the bill, one a man and one a woman? And you're both so good-looking! It's a natural!"

Roxy stared into her coffee cup.

"And I'll pay you a salary," Jill said. "_And_ . . . I'll help you look for your father."

"How are you going to do that?"

"I don't know," Jill admitted, "but you've been looking alone for a long time. Maybe you can use some help."

Roxy thought it over.

"So what do you say?" Jill asked.

"Your partner is going along with this?" Roxy asked.

"Derek is fine," Jill said. "Look, this is between us girls. Never mind what Derek or Bill will think. So . . . what's your answer?"

Roxy hesitated, then said, "I'll sign on, for now. And if I don't find my father here, I'll go to Denver with you. But after that . . . who knows?"

"Who knows, indeed," Jill said. She raised her coffee cup. "Here's to us girls."

Roxy raised her cup, as well, wondering if she was making the right decision.

***

The word got around the grounds fast that the Lady Gunsmith had signed on to join the circus.

Les Collier decided it had to be because she was looking for him. He was going to have to do something about her.

Something drastic.

***

Derek Pomerantz knocked on the door of Bill Weatherly's wagon. When the sharpshooter opened it, Bill showed him the whiskey bottle and two glasses.

"Come on in," Weatherly said.

Pomerantz entered and immediately poured two drinks, handing one to Weatherly.

"How are you doin'?" he asked.

"I'm fine," Weatherly said, sitting. He had a bed and a table with two chairs in the wagon. Also a chest where he kept his clothes. His guns hung on the wall on a rack.

"This is the first time you've ever lost," Pomerantz pointed out. "And to a girl."

"A woman, I think," Weatherly said. "Ain't nothin' girlie about her."

Pomerantz nodded in agreement. "Have you heard that she signed on?" he asked. "Jill pushed her, and she did it."

"You should be happy about that," Weatherly said. "She's going to be a big draw."

"I'm worried about the effect on you."

"Don't worry about me, Derek," Weatherly said, "I'm fine."

"You think it was a fluke that she beat you?"

"That woman is no fluke."

"So you think she can beat you again," Pomerantz said. "What if it happens again in Denver?"

"Then she'll be five hundred dollars richer, won't she?"

"Okay," Pomerantz said, "let's change the subject. What's going on between you and Jill?"

"What do you mean?" Weatherly asked. "We're married."

"Yeah, but are you really married?" Pomerantz asked. "I don't see her spending many nights in here with you."

"Well, Derek," Weatherly said, "that's our business, ain't it?"

"You had Lulu Mae in here a few nights ago," Pomerantz said. "What the hell were you doing with her?"

"What do you think I was doing with her?" Weatherly asked.

"She has a beard, man!"

"Have you seen the rest of her?"

"Come on, Bill," Pomerantz said. "Who's next? Rosita?"

"What's wrong with Rosita?"

"She's the fat lady!"

"She has beautiful skin," Weatherly said. "Look, Derek, if you want to sleep with Jill and she says yes, go ahead. Don't go looking for problems in my marriage to justify it. Jill and me, we got an understanding."

Pomerantz sighed. "It doesn't matter. She's not interested, anyway."

"Then move on, Derek," Weatherly said. "I'm telling you, Lulu Mae may have a beard, but in bed she'll change your life."

"Ahh," Pomerantz said, rubbing his hand over his face, "I can't get past that beard." He paused a moment, then poured two more drinks. "Tell me again about the fat lady?"

Chapter Nineteen

Jill told Roxy they didn't have a wagon she could move into yet, but they would by the time they were ready to pull out and head for Denver. So Roxy went back to her hotel, her arms aching, but with five hundred dollars in her pocket.

When she got to her room she laid the rifle aside and removed her gunbelt, hanging it on the bedpost. Then she sat on the bed and pulled off her boots. She leaned back on her hands and took a deep breath. Now, with the money safely in her pocket, she was free to think about other things: Jill's offer of work, Bill Weatherly's stupid remarks about killing men, and Johnny Steel's charming smile.

Jill was right about one thing. Another five hundred prize money would be very welcome. And she didn't know how the woman planned to help her look for her father, but she had to admit that some help would be welcome.

Robert Pinkerton's report about Blackhawk had come from another rumor. Usually when she followed a rumor and found out it was untrue, she moved on. But since the information had come from the Pinkerton Agency, she was willing to give it some time.

Bill Weatherly was a man who spent his life shooting at targets. He had never faced a man with a gun—or a woman, for that matter—and if he had to, he'd probably freeze and get killed. Because of his dumb remarks, she was glad she had beaten him.

She wasn't quite as happy about beating Johnny Steel. But he was an experienced gambler, and those men knew how to pick up a stake. He had probably already moved on to the next idea.

At that moment someone knocked on her door. She grabbed her gun from the bedpost and carried it with her to the door. She half expected to find Jill Weatherly in the hall, but as it turned out, it was Steel.

"I missed you at the tent," he said, holding out a bottle of champagne and two glasses. "I thought you might like to celebrate your victory."

"That's very sweet," she said. "Come on in."

"Are you sure?" he asked, looking up and down the hall. "You're not worried about your reputation?"

"For a glass of champagne," she said, "I'll risk it."

Truth be told if she had ever had a glass of champagne before, she couldn't remember the taste.

Steel entered the room and Roxy closed the door. As she reholstered her pistol Steel popped the cork on the champagne and filled the two glasses.

"Here you go," he said, handing her one. "Congratulations on a well-earned victory. I'm sure your arms are as sore as mine are."

"Thank you. Yes, they are."

"I'm more used to hefting cards than a rifle, I have to admit."

"You did pretty well, I'd say," she told him. "If you're a better gambler than you are a marksman, you've gotta be pretty damn good."

"If I'm pretty good why did I need a stake, is that what you're thinking?"

"Maybe . . ."

"Every gambler hits a dry spell," he said. "I hit mine about three weeks ago, and it's still going. I've just got to play my way out of it, and for that I need a stake." He raised his glass in the air. "And that's the way it goes, sometimes. I just thought I'd take a chance, today, but you . . . you didn't give anybody a chance. You don't miss, do you?"

"I can't afford to miss," she said.

"Not with a name like Lady Gunsmith, huh?" Steel asked. "And I guess you know the Gunsmith, don't you?"

"I do," she said. "He taught me most of what I know."

"And what he didn't teach you?"

"Comes naturally."

"What else comes naturally?" he asked, giving her that charming smile.

She decided to be bold.

"Why don't you take off your clothes and I'll show you."

Chapter Twenty

Roxy decided to help him.

"This is what you came up here for, isn't it?" she asked, removing his jacket.

"Well," he admitted, letting the jacket drop to the floor, "I had hopes—"

She cut him off by pulling his head down and kissing him. She was a tall girl, and he was only slightly taller, so it was a good fit. While they kissed she unbuttoned his shirt and slid her hands inside, rubbing them over his bare chest. He put his arms around her, pulled her close and the kiss intensified. Then, suddenly, she disengaged and stepped back.

"What happened?" he asked. "Was it . . . all right?"

"It was a test," she said.

"What kind of test?"

"To see if we fit together."

"And?"

"You passed," she said.

"So . . . what's next?"

"The bed," she said. "After you get undressed."

"I started to get under—"

She closed the space between them and kissed him again, this time peeling his shirt off during the kiss. Then she stepped back as the shirt fluttered to the floor.

"Wha—" he said.

"I'm sorry," she said. "It's that damn charming smile. It just makes me want to kiss you."

"Well, thank—" he started, smiling again.

"Damn!" She charged him and kissed him, undoing his belt. This time, though, he stopped the kiss and stepped back.

"Okay," he said, "let's get undressed and into bed."

"Just stop smiling!" she insisted.

"I'll try!"

He managed to remove his boots, trousers and underwear without her charging him again. When he was naked his erection poked out at her and it was Roxy who smiled, because she liked it. It was like his smile, charming.

He watched while she removed her clothing, and when she was naked he stared. Roxy was full-bodied, with large, rounded breasts, smooth skin and the requisite freckles of a redhead. The tangle of hair between her legs was like burnt copper.

"My God," he breathed, "you're beautiful!"

This time they closed the space between them together, locked in a hot kiss, their bodies pressed tightly to each other. She could feel his hard cock trapped between them, and knew he could feel her nipples against his chest.

She broke the kiss, turned him so that his back was to the edge of the bed, and pushed him so he fell onto it. On his back, with his hard dick sticking up, he was in a perfect position for her.

She got on her knees between his legs, which were hanging over the bottom of the bed, and wasted no time taking his penis into her mouth. He groaned and reached down to wrap his hands in her red hair and hold her there. But there was no danger of her pulling away this time. Not until she was done.

Her head began to bob up and down as she sucked him avidly, enjoying the way his smooth cock glided in and out of her mouth. She hated those ugly, veiny things many men had between their legs. Sucking John Steel's cock was a pleasure.

"Jesus," he said, "I'm gonna—"

"No, you're not," she said, letting him slide from her mouth. She squeezed his cock at the base, managing to stave off his eruption. "Not yet, anyway."

She stood, got on the bed with him and said, "slide over."

"Yes, Ma'am." He moved up so that his head was on the pillow, and now his legs were fully on the bed.

She mounted him, let the head of his cock slide up and down her moist pussy lips for a few seconds before sitting down on him and taking him inside.

"God!" he cried out.

"No God," she said to him. "This is just between you and me."

It had been some time since Roxy was with a man, so she was determined to enjoy this for as long as he lasted. She bounced up and down on him, bracing herself by pressing her hands against his sternum so she could get good height before coming back down. Every time she did he grunted, and she could see from his expression, the concentration on his face that he was doing his best to hold off before finishing.

Abruptly, she reversed her position, turning around so that her back was to him, but all the while keeping him inside her. She enjoyed the way it felt when she rotated, and then she began bouncing up and down on him again, this time with her hands pressed down on the bed, between his legs.

"Jesus, girl," he said, "you're killin' me . . . don't stop!"

And she didn't, not until he let out a great big bellow and she felt him explode inside of her, like a million tiny hot needles. But she continued to move on him, as he remained hard long enough for her to find her own release. She hissed, letting the air out from between her lips instead of yelling, and then lifted her butt and let his cock pop free, glistening from her juices.

She collapsed on her back next to him, reached over and took his cock in her hand. It was still partially hard.

"Gimme a minute," he gasped, "and we'll do it again."

"Okay," she agreed, "but just once more, and then I've got to get some sleep."

***

The second time she let him fuck her while she was on her back, a position most men preferred. She raised her knees so he could achieve maximum penetration, and then he exploded inside of her again. This time he collapsed next to her, on his side.

"Jesus, woman, you're amazing at everything you do, aren't you?"

"I try to be," she said. "But now it's time for you to leave."

"I thought we were going to sleep?"

"We are," she said, "in our own beds." She didn't like a man to remain in her bed when she was done with him. She couldn't sleep that way.

"What about tomorrow morning—"

"I've got to be at the circus," she said. "I start working there tomorrow."

"But . . . when will I see you again?"

"I don't know, Johnny," she said. "In a few days the circus moves on to Denver, and I'll be with it."

"So . . . we're done?"

"Probably." She slapped him on the ass. "Now get yourself dressed and out of here, and thanks for coming by."

Chapter Twenty-One

The next morning she woke in need of a bath. She liked the way John Steel smelled, but that didn't mean she wanted the scent on her all day. So she had the clerk in the hotel drawn her a bath, then had breakfast and headed for the circus grounds.

When she got there the circus was in full operation. Families were walking around, playing the games, laughing at the clowns and looking at animals in cages. Roxy went to where she and Jill had coffee together, found several circus people there sitting and drinking. She didn't recognize any of them, so she went to get herself a cup of coffee.

"Excuse me," someone said.

She turned, saw a woman with a full, mature body, big breasts, lovely skin—and a beard.

"This area is only for people who work at the circus," she said.

"You've got to be Lulu Mae," Roxy said.

"I don't know if I have to be, but I am," she admitted. "Who are you?"

"I'm Roxy Doyle," she said, sticking her hand out. "I won the sharpshooting competition yesterday, and now I work here."

"Oh," Lulu Mae said, taking Roxy's hand and shaking it, "you're the one who beat Bill at his own game."

"I suppose you could put it that way."

"Well, all right, then," Lulu Mae said, "come and sit so we can get to know one another."

They walked to a table and sat across from each other. Roxy was amazed at how full the woman's beard was, and how beautiful she was in every other aspect. She had the most piercing violet colored eyes Roxy had ever seen.

"You're very beautiful," Roxy said.

"I'll take that as a compliment, since you obviously know what you're talkin' about. You're gorgeous!"

"Thank you."

"How long do you think you'll be workin' here?" the bearded lady asked.

"I don't have any idea," Roxy said. "Up until yesterday it never occurred to me to work at a circus. Why? How long do most people work here?"

"Well, we have a few long timers, like me, Lucas the strongman, some of the clowns, Archibald the lion tamer, like them. Others come and go pretty quick."

"Do you mind if I ask you about, uh . . ."

"My beard? And why I don't shave it off?"

"Yes—no offense meant."

"None taken. Fact is, I have shaved it off a time or two, but then it comes back even fuller than ever. If I keep doin' that, it'll grow to the floor!" The woman laughed. "Seriously, this is who I am. I'm the bearded lady. If I went anywhere else, I'd be a freak. Here I'm accepted, and . . . I get paid for bein' me."

"But . . . what about, you know, men?"

"Darlin'," Lulu Mae said, "I had my pick of men. They're real curious, you know? Fact is, once we're in bed and I'm naked, they forget all about the beard. Or they go after the, you know, other one." She pointed down below the table.

"Can I ask you some more questions?" Roxy asked. "About others who work here?"

"Sure, honey, go ahead. I'll fill you in."

"Jill told me about Bill Weatherly sleeping around with the women who work here."

"Includin' me?"

"Well, yes."

"It's true," she said. "If Bill wasn't the sharpshooter around here, he'd be a whore."

"And nobody minds?"

"Fact is," Lulu Mae said, "he's damn good in bed. Why would a woman mind that?"

"But . . . he's married to Jill."

"Oh, they have the same appetites," Lulu Mae said. "That's why they're together."

"So she sleeps around, too?"

"She does," Lulu Mae said, "and not only with men."

"You mean—"

"I mean watch your step around her," Lulu Mae said. Then she studied Roxy and rubbed her jaw. "Wonder which of them will get you into bed first? Maybe I'll start a pool."

"Fact is," Roxy responded, "I try not to sleep with married people."

"Then you'll be the first one to throw money into the pool!"

They were still laughing when Jill Weatherly came along.

PART TWO

THE CIRCUS

Chapter Twenty-Two

"Roxy! You're here. I was hoping you wouldn't change your mind."

"I haven't," Roxy said. "Lulu Mae was just filling me in on some of your people."

"She was, eh?" Jill looked at Lulu Mae. "Don't you have some work to do?"

Lulu Mae stood up. "Time to be the freak on display. See you later, Roxy."

"I don't know what she told you," Jill said as the bearded lady walked away, "but you've got to take it with a grain of salt."

"All she told me was you and your husband have an understanding," Roxy said. "Which, by the way, you pretty much told me, yourself. You don't care who the other sleeps with."

"As long as we come back to each other every time," Jill added. "That's true—but it's also our business."

"Understood," Roxy said. "I won't mention it again. But while I'm here working for you, you have to understand that I still have to tend to my business."

"Finding your father."

"Right."

"And I said I'd help," Jill reminded her. "I haven't forgot. If you give me his description, I'll make sure everybody in the circus knows it. If he shows up, we'll see him."

"I can only tell you what he looked like the last time I saw him," Roxy explained. "I was eleven."

"That'll have to do."

Roxy told Jill what she remembered. Her father was a tall, rangy man with brown hair, and clean shaven.

"He could have a beard now, for all I know, and gained weight."

"Then how will you recognize him?"

"I just will."

"We'll do the best we can," Jill said. "Now, about you and Bill shooting together. You two are going to have to work out a show."

"He's the pro," Roxy said. "I'll just be guided by him."

"Then let me take you to his wagon so the two of you can work it out. This way."

Roxy got up and followed Jill across the circus grounds to the other side, where all the wagons were situated. Some were empty, their contents having been unpacked and used. Others held animals, or people.

Jill walked up to one and knocked on the door. When it opened, Bill Weatherly looked out. It was the first time Roxy had seen him without his gun on—or his hat, for that matter.

"Oh, hey, Jill," he said.

"Bill. Here's Roxy Doyle. You have to work out a routine with her."

"That shouldn't be a problem," Weatherly said. "Come on inside."

Roxy hesitated. She wondered if Jill was leading her to Bill the way a lamb is led to the slaughter? Was she expected to go into his wagon and have sex with him?

"I'll be back later to walk you around a bit," Jill said. "And don't worry about the rumors. He won't touch you unless you want him to."

As Roxy entered the wagon Weatherly closed the door, then turned to face her.

"Rumors?"

"About you and the women in the circus."

"Oh. Who have you been talking to? Jill?"

"And Lulu Mae."

"Ah yes," Weatherly said, with a fond smile, "Lulu Mae."

"A lady with a beard?" Roxy asked.

"You've seen the rest of her," Weatherly said. "And behind that beard is a beautiful face. Would you like a drink? Or some coffee?"

"Coffee would be fine."

"Comin' up."

He poured a cup from a pot on the stove and brought it over to her.

"Sit anywhere," he said.

There was a bed, a chest, and a chair. She chose the chair. He perched on the chest. She found it encouraging that he hadn't sat on the bed.

The interior of the wagon was rather cramped, and she wondered . . .

"You live here with Jill?"

"Oh, no," he said, "this is my private sanctuary. This is where I clean my guns, work out my routines—sort of like an office on wheels."

"Ah."

"No, Jill and I share another wagon," Weatherly said.

"And when you sleep with other women you bring them here?" Roxy asked.

"Oh, no," he said, "I bring them to our wagon. The bed is bigger."

"You sleep with other women in the bed you share with Jill?" Roxy asked.

"Well, sure," he said. "When she sleeps with other men—or women—she takes them there."

Up to then it had only been inferred that Jill liked men and women. Now her husband had confirmed it.

She ignored the remark.

"So, let's get to know one another," Weatherly said. He leaned forward, with his elbows on his knees.

"How do you mean?"

"Not that way," he said, looking at the bed. "I just mean, let's get acquainted. Jill told me you're Lady Gunsmith."

"Yes, I am."

"And that you're looking for your father."

"Also right."

"What's his name?"

"Gavin Doyle."

"What's he do?"

"He's a bounty hunter," she said. "A famous one."

91

"Sorry," he said, "I'm not well informed when it comes to that world."

"That's okay."

"Are you a bounty hunter?"

"No. I'm just looking for him. If I was a bounty hunter, an experienced tracker, I'd probably be having more luck."

"What will you do when you find him?" Weatherly asked.

Roxy hesitated. "I don't know. I mean, I'm not sure. Get to know him again, I guess."

"And you think he'll be here? In the circus?"

"No," she said, "the word I got is that he's in Blackhawk. You all just happened to be here, too."

"I see." He sat back. "Okay, then. Let's come up with a routine."

"Oh no," she said.

"Why?"

"You said we should get acquainted," she said. "It's your turn. Tell me about you and Jill."

Chapter Twenty-Three

"Jill used to run a carnival. I worked for Pomerantz's circus. When they joined forces, we joined forces, too."

"When did you get married?"

"Weeks after we met."

"Why?"

"Because we're alike," he said. "We have the same needs, and wants."

"I thought you were going to say because you fell in love?"

"That, too," he said, "but it was more than that. Nobody understands us like we understand each other."

"So the other people in the circus, they know this? Lulu Mae knew when she slept with you?"

"Of course. And Rosita—"

"Rosita?"

"The fat lady."

"You slept with the fat lady?"

"She has beautiful skin—and a beautiful soul."

"And what about the men here?"

"Well," he said, "Jill's real particular. I think that's why she tried women."

"Like Lulu Mae?"

"Oh, no," Weatherly said, "Lulu Mae likes men, not women. Same with Rosita. But there are a few, some of the lady clowns—"

"You have lady clowns?"

He smiled. "All kinds of clowns."

"So if Jill is a part owner, aren't you?"

"No," he said. "I just work here, like you."

"When did you know you were good with guns?" she asked.

"I was twelve when I picked up my first gun," he said. "It felt so natural, and I was able to hit anything I pointed at."

"Are you fast?"

"No," he said, "you've seen me shoot. I'm very deliberate. I'm not a fast gun, I'm a trick shooter. If I faced someone like you, I'd get killed."

"It's good that you know that."

"Oh, believe me, I do. I tried it once, when I was young and feeling my oats. Faced a man and he shot me. I almost died then. I'm not looking forward to doing that, again."

"I don't blame you."

"Have you killed a lot of men?"

"Quite a few."

"But you're still so young."

"I started early."

"And have you been shot, yourself?"

"Twice."

"Ever almost died?"

She shook her head.

"I haven't had a wound that serious, yet."

"Yet?"

"The life I lead, I'll have one, or more. Hopefully, I'll survive them all."

"Why not hang up your guns?"

"It's too late for that," she said. "I have a name. It would follow me everywhere."

"Not here," he said.

"Why not?"

"There are people here who are hiding," he said. "Nobody's found them, yet."

"Hiding from what?"

"An old life."

"Are you?"

"No," he said, "this is me. This is who I am."

"Then who?"

"Why do you think Lulu Mae keeps her beard, or Rosita keeps her weight?"

"So they look different."

He nodded.

"And Jill?"

"Jill is Jill."

"Well," Roxy said, "this is very interesting. I'll have to give it some thought. But for now, I suppose we'd better work on that routine."

"Right, right," he said. "I have this idea about us shooting things off of each other . . ."

***

Roxy found Bill Weatherly much friendlier and, yes,

95

much more charming than he had been during the competition. She assumed that he preferred to keep himself away from his competitors so he could focus on what he was doing.

She also found everything he told her about the circus people interesting. How many of them, she wondered, were hiding from old lives? And who were they besides, the bearded lady and the fat lady?

Next, she found Weatherly's idea for a routine interesting. But they were going to have to trust each other's ability with a gun completely in order for it to work.

"Do you think we can do this?" Weatherly asked.

"I think so. Do we have to do it tonight for the first time?"

"Well," he suggested, "we could go right now and rehearse it."

"That sounds like a good idea."

"Okay," he said, "let me get my gunbelt and my hat."

He put them both on and led the way to the door. As they went out together there was a shot, and a bullet lodged in the door right between them.

"Duck!" he shouted, tackling her and taking her to the ground as a second shot came.

Twenty-Four

From the ground they both rolled in opposite directions, but ended up underneath the wagon together, their guns in their hands.

"What the hell—" Weatherly swore. "Who's shooting at us?"

"I don't know," she said, "but thanks for taking me down when you did. That second shot might have got me."

"You think they were shooting at you?" he asked.

"Think about it," she said. "Does anybody have any reason to shoot at you?"

He did think about it, and could not come up with an answer right away.

"Okay," she said, "maybe a jealous husband or boyfriend, but it's more likely somebody recognized me and decided to take a try."

"From hiding?" he asked. "Who wants a reputation bushwhacking people?"

"That all depends on who you're bushwhacking," Roxy answered, still looking around for a target.

"Are they gone?" he asked. "Or still out there?"

"That's what I'm trying to decide," she said.

***

Les Collier swore at himself.

He hadn't expected Bill Weatherly to come out of the wagon first. In fact, Weatherly shouldn't have come out, at all. Doyle was visiting him, so when they were finished doing whatever they were doing, she should have come out alone.

Weatherly's appearance had thrown off his shot. And then him taking her down saved her from the second one. And after that one he couldn't afford another, so he fled. Even if anyone had seen him they wouldn't recognize him. He wasn't in his clown persona, and that's how the circus people knew him. It had been a long time—well, weeks— since anyone had seen him out of make-up.

And he wanted to keep it that way.

***

"I think it's safe," Roxy said.

They rolled out from under the wagon and stood up, careful to look around.

"Nobody," she said.

"This is kind of far from the rest of the circus," he said. "For the sake of privacy. And with the calliope going, nobody heard those shots. I'm sure of it."

She stared straight ahead of her.

"What are you looking for?" he asked.

"Someplace those shots would have come from," she said.

"He could have been on top of another wagon," he suggested.

"That's true. But why did he miss?"

"I pulled you down," he pointed out.

"Yes, but how did he miss the first time. We were sitting ducks."

"I guess it depends on which one of us he wanted," Weatherly said.

"It had to be me."

"But I came out first," Weatherly said, "and he fired."

"Maybe he thought I was coming out first," she said, "or alone. He was all ready to fire, and he did. Only when he saw it was you he didn't have time to alter the first shot."

"I don't know," he said. "I'm thinking about what you said about jealousy."

"A husband or boyfriend?"

"Or something else."

"Like what?" she asked.

"Well," he said, "this is probably wrong, but Pomerantz—"

"Your wife's partner?"

He nodded.

"He wants to be more than that."

"And you think he'd kill you to get you out of the way?" she asked.

"I don't know," he said. "I'm just thinking about it now."

"But . . . you're his headliner, aren't you?"

"I was," Weatherly said, "but maybe now . . . you'll be."

"I don't want to be a headliner," she said. "I just want to make some money, and find my father. That's the only reason I'm doing this."

"So what now?"

"We might as well go and work on the routine."

"But what about being shot at?" he asked. "Shouldn't we tell somebody?"

She thought a moment, then said, "No. Let the shooter wonder what we're doing, why we're not reporting it. Let him think a while."

"Him?"

"Or her," Roxy said, "but I think it's more likely a 'him.'"

"What about Jill?" Weatherly asked. "Should we tell her?"

"She's your wife," Roxy said. "Do you tell her everything?"

Weatherly hesitated. "Well, not everything."

"Leave it to me," she suggested, "since I think they were shooting at me. If I think she should know, I'll tell her."

"Fine," he said. "I'll leave it up to you."

Chapter Twenty-Five

Roxy and Weatherly spent over an hour in the big tent, rehearsing their routine. Neither of them ever missed, so by the end of the rehearsal they were confident enough in each other's abilities that they agreed to go ahead with it.

They didn't think that anyone was watching them, as there was a lot going on around them, other rehearsals, acrobats, clowns, the lion tamer—as well as scenery being erected. There was banging, sawing, roaring, and the snap of the lion tamer's whip.

And there were two people who were watching them very intently . . .

***

Jill stood off to one side, watching the two sharpshooters go through their paces. From what she could see, the act was going to be good, very good. But she hoped that, at some point, they'd come up with something spectacular.

She was also watching to see if anything had developed between them in the short time they were together. From what she could see, the two never touched each other—and probably hadn't. Jill thought Roxy was a smart girl, and able to resist her husband's charms. Most of the women in the circus weren't that smart, or simply didn't care. They just wanted to be with Weatherly, even if it was only one time.

Jill married him because they were the same, and no matter who else came and went in their lives, they would end up together. In that way jealousy never entered into their relationship, because lust was forgiven, overruled by love.

And damn, could the two of them shoot!

***

Collier was once again Lester the Clown, and he was sitting way up in the stands, in the shadows, watching Roxy Doyle rehearse with Bill Weatherly. He wondered why an alarm hadn't been raised after the shooting? Hadn't they told anyone that it happened? And if not, why not?

He had heard through the circus grapevine that Doyle was in town looking for her father, Gavin Doyle. So now he knew for certain they were related. What he didn't need was for them to get together and hunt him. That meant he had to get rid of her before that happened. And if the bounty hunter wasn't already in Blackhawk, maybe the circus could up and move on to Denver before he got there.

But first things first.

Kill Roxy Doyle.

Chapter Twenty-Six

The rehearsal ended when Roxy and Bill Weatherly agreed that they had the routine down perfectly—or as perfectly as they could get it.

"Want to get something to eat?" Weatherly asked.

"Yes," she said, "but I'll do it in town. I still have something to attend to."

"Look for your father?"

She nodded.

"I wish you luck, then," he said, "and I'll see you tonight. We go on at eight, so get here by seven."

"I'll see you then."

He nodded and they went their separate ways.

***

Roxy walked to town, stopped in a café for a quick bite to eat. Then she made a circuit of the streets of Blackhawk, keeping an eagle eye out for her father.

She realized while talking to Jill that she really was going to have to depend on her instincts to identify her father. The memory of an 11-year-old was not going to be reliable.

So as she walked she tried to bring that memory into focus, and age it. What did Gavin Doyle look like now? Was he heavier? More gray? Maybe bald? Had he ever married, again? Probably not. The life of a bounty hunter didn't usually include marriage.

She felt the man behind her before she turned, but no impending danger.

"Any luck?"

She turned to face Sheriff Kyle Marks.

"In findin' your father, I mean," Marks said.

"No," she said, "no luck."

"I heard you had some luck at the circus, though," he said. "It's all over town that Lady Gunsmith beat the circus sharpshooter."

"That wasn't luck," she said. "I was just better than he was."

"Oh," he said, "well, that must have disappointed the circus people."

"Not so much."

"Really? That's odd."

"And they offered me a job."

"Ah," he said, "so you're not leavin' town."

"Not until the circus does."

"That's good."

"Is it? Why?"

"I uh, thought maybe we'd get to know each other better. You know, have supper together?"

"I don't think so."

"Why not?" he asked. "Am I too old? Not handsome enough? I mean, I know I'm not handsome—"

"You're a lawman."

That stopped Marks.

"What's that got to do with anythin'?"

"I don't like lawmen."

Marks looked puzzled.

"Is that because your father's a bounty hunter?"

"No," she said, "I just haven't had much luck with lawmen. They tend to think I'm always lookin' for trouble, and I'm not."

"Trouble looks for you, though, doesn't it?"

She hesitated, then said, "Well, it tends to find me. I don't know if it's actually looking for me."

"See," Sheriff Marks said, "if you were with me, it wouldn't."

"I appreciate the offer, Sheriff," she said, "but I'm going to pass."

"Well . . . okay," he said. "I guess . . . if trouble does manage to find you, let me know."

"I will."

He walked away and didn't look back. She hoped he was done inviting her to meals.

***

She continued walking around town, and eventually saw a man with a badge coming toward her. It wasn't the sheriff though, it was the deputy.

The young, handsome, happily married deputy.

"Hello, Deputy Starrett."

"Miss Doyle," Andy the Deputy said.

"How are you?"

"I'm fine," he said, shifting his feet nervously.

"And your lovely wife and son? How are they?"

"They're—they're good."

"Does your wife know how lucky she is?" she asked, touching his face. "I mean, to have such a handsome husband?"

He blushed. "I hope so."

She couldn't help herself. He was so sweet and . . . young.

"And in bed?" Roxy asked. "Does she keep you happy in bed?"

She noticed his eyes shifting about, probably to see if anyone was looking at them. People were walking by, but very few were paying them any attention. And if they were, they were looking at her, not him.

"Hmm? Do you keep her happy?"

"We—we have a son," he stammered.

"Well," she said, running her hand down the front of his shirt, "that just means you had sex once. It doesn't even mean you enjoyed it." She couldn't help herself, she was having fun with him.

"Well . . ."

"Do you go to whores?" she asked. "For the enjoyable sex?"

"No!" he said. "No, I—I'm a deputy!"

"I see," she said. "Deputy's don't have sex for enjoyment?"

"Deputies don't go to whores," he said, firmly. "And married men shouldn't go to whores."

"Why not?"

"Because they're married!" He was almost indignant.

"But what if they're not happy?"

Suddenly, he got angry. "I am happy!"

"Sure you are."

He brushed her hand away and said, "I have rounds to make, Miss Doyle."

"Well," she said, as he walked away, "if you change your mind about sex for enjoyment and still don't want a whore, come and see me. I like handsome young boys."

He walked away faster, and she smiled, knowing she was being a bitch and not understanding why.

Chapter Twenty-Seven

When Roxy got back to the circus the grounds were crowded with people. There was a line waiting to buy tickets into the big top, where she and Weatherly were scheduled to perform. He had told her to come back at seven, but it was six when she got herself a cup of coffee and sat down.

"You mind?" Lulu Mae asked, approaching the table.

"No, I don't mind."

The bearded lady sat opposite her.

"You were amazing yesterday," she said.

"Thanks."

"It was fun, seeing Bill get beat by a woman."

"He doesn't seem to mind."

"That's only because you were so good," she said. "He got beat by somebody better. There's nothing he can do about that."

"Can I ask you a question?" Roxy asked.

"Sure, why not?"

"It's about sex."

Lulu Mae smiled beautifully behind that heavy beard.

"My favorite subject," she said.

"Why did you have sex with Weatherly?"

"Uh-oh," Lulu Mae said, "are you interested in him that way?"

"No," Roxy said. "I'm curious. I like Jill, and she's married to him."

"Don't worry about Jill," Lulu Mae said. "She can take care of herself. You like her?"

"Yes, I do. Why?"

"Nobody likes her."

"Nobody?"

"Well," Lulu Mae said, "most of the girls. Wait, here's Rosita." She waved to the fat woman, who waddled over to the table.

This was the first time Roxy had seen Rosita. She was obese, with folds of fat around her neck, her arms and legs. Roxy couldn't see the rest of her body, it was covered by a robe.

"Hey, Lu," Rosita said.

"Sit down," Lulu Mae said, "talk to Roxy Doyle and I'll get you some coffee."

"Thanks."

Rosita sat and sighed. Every movement seemed to be difficult for her.

Roxy studied her, trying to picture the woman having sex with Bill Weatherly, or any man, for that matter.

"So you're Roxy, huh? The Lady Gunsmith who beat Bill?"

"That's right."

Rosita put her hand out and Roxy shook it.

"Welcome," she said.

"Thanks."

"You're performing with Bill tonight, right?"

"Yes, I am."

Lulu Mae came back and put the coffee cup down in front of Rosita.

"Thanks," the fat lady said.

Lulu Mae sat next to her.

"I didn't answer your question," Lulu Mae said.

"What question?" Rosita asked.

"She wants to know why I had sex with Bill."

"Really?" Rosita looked at Roxy. "Did you have sex with him already?"

"Oh, no."

"Are you gonna?"

"No. I'm just curious."

"She likes Jill," Lulu Mae said to Rosita. "She wonders why she's married to Bill if he sleeps around."

"You like Jill?" Rosita asked.

"I do, yes."

"I told her hardly anybody does," Lulu said.

"That's true," Rosita said. "She's kind of a bitch."

"Then why do you stay?" Roxy asked.

"She's a boss bitch," Rosita said, "and where else could I work?"

"So," Lulu Mae said, "to answer the question, I wanted to have sex with Bill. To see if he was as good as he says he is."

"And was he?"

"Oh, yeah," Lulu Mae said, "he's real good."

"And how many times did you have sex with him?" Roxy asked.

"Once," Lulu Mae said. "That's all it took to find out."

Roxy looked at Rosita.

"Once for me, too," she said. "I don't know who was more curious, me or him. But once was enough. It was good, but it was enough."

"Why don't you do it and see?" Lulu Mae asked.

"He doesn't appeal to me that way," Roxy said, "and I have to work with him. If anything gets in the way of what we're doing, one of us could get shot."

Lulu Mae and Rosita exchanged a glance, and the bearded lady said, "That makes sense."

"Probably the only thing around here that does."

Roxy saw two little people—midgets? Dwarves? She wasn't sure—approach the food table. She'd only seen one or two before in her life. One of these was male, and one female.

"What do they do?" she asked.

Lulu Mae turned to see who she meant.

"Oh, they're clowns," Lulu Mae said. "Coco and Kiki."

"Really?"

"Those are their clown names. They're real names—I forget their real names. Rosita?"

"I don't remember real names around here," Rosita said. "To me they're Coco and Kiki."

"Which one's the girl?"

"Kiki," Lulu Mae said.

"Are they together?" Roxy asked.

"You mean married?" Rosita asked. "Oh, yeah, but that didn't stop Kiki."

"Stop her from what?"

"What are we talkin' about?" Lulu Mae asked. "Stop her from having sex with Bill."

"Come on!"

"It's true," Rosita said.

"And you're going to tell me her husband, Coco, didn't mind?"

"Shhh," Lulu Mae said, "he doesn't know."

"What?" Roxy asked. "The word must get around here fast."

"Well," Rosita said, "let's just say he doesn't want to know."

"And did she do it just once?" Roxy asked.

"Oh yeah," Lulu Mae said. "Just once. Bill likes to do it just once with each girl, and then he goes home and has sex with his wife all night."

"Wait a minute," Roxy said. "I just put it together. They're Bill and Jill?"

Lulu Mae and Rosita laughed.

"Ain't that funny?" Rosita asked.

Roxy started to laugh, too, because yes, it was funny.

The whole place was funny!

Chapter Twenty-Eight

The routine went perfectly.

The finale had them facing each other, drawing, and each shot the worn-out holster off the other's hip. She wasn't about to let him shoot her own holster. Weatherly had plenty of extras. The crowd went wild.

They bowed, waved to the crowd, and walked off as the clowns came running out. The two little clowns run right by her.

"Are they midgets or dwarves?" she asked Weatherly when they got outside.

"What? Who?"

"The little clowns," she said. "Midgets or dwarves?"

"Why does that matter?" he asked.

"I don't want to insult anyone."

"They're dwarves."

"Thanks."

"You want to get a drink?" Weatherly asked. "Or coffee? To celebrate our first performance?"

"No, that's okay," Roxy said. "I'll see you tomorrow."

"Hey," he said, as she walked away.

"What?"

"Did I do something?"

"Not a thing." She turned and walked away, strapping her own holster on.

Lester the Clown saw Roxy and Weatherly walk out of the tent, and followed. He couldn't kill her, not right there with the grounds full of people. But he wanted to see if she went with him, or if they separated. So he watched while they exchanged a few words, then went their separate ways. He didn't follow her, because she was Lady Gunsmith. She'd know if she was being followed.

Another time, he thought, as he watched her walk away.

***

"Roxy!"

She turned, saw Jill running after her. When she reached Roxy she gave her a hug.

"That was great!" she said, releasing her.

"Thanks."

"The crowd loved it. I knew this would work."

"You're a smart woman."

"Yes, I am," Jill said, happily.

"I'm not going to have sex with your husband."

"What?"

"It's not going to happen."

"That's . . . well, that's fine . . . why are you telling me this?"

"Because I get the feeling you want me to."

"Why would I want you to?"

"I don't know," Roxy said. "You don't seem to mind when he sleeps with everyone else. So wanting me to may be the next step."

"Look," Jill said, "my relationship with my husband is my business."

"Right," Roxy said, "so don't try to get me involved. I've got my own life to live."

"Finding your father?"

"Yes."

"What makes you think he's even still alive?"

"Because . . . if he was dead, I'd know."

"How?"

"I just would."

"Okay," Jill said, "look, all I want from you is the best you can give me when you're on. Can you do that?"

"I can."

"Then don't worry about who my husband sleeps with, or who I sleep with."

"Fine."

"Fine."

"I'll see you tomorrow." Jill turned, then stepped back. "I might have a wagon for you by then."

"Okay."

She turned, and this time walked away.

Chapter Twenty-Nine

Roxy left the circus grounds while it was still busy there. She went back to her hotel, but before she entered the lobby she stopped and looked across the street, where there was a saloon called The Red Door. Abruptly, she stepped into the street, crossed, and went through the batwing doors—one of which was red.

She didn't stop inside, just proceeded to the bar, as the conversation in the place waned a bit. Men watched her walk, then went back to their games, or friends, or drinks.

There was room at the bar without the men there moving out of her way, but nevertheless they moved. Many of them had seen her shoot, and knew who she was.

"Beer," she told the bartender.

"Comin' up," the middle-aged man said. He drew the beer and set it in front of her. "Uh, you ain't lookin' for anybody in here, are ya, Lady Gunsmith?"

"That's Miss Doyle to you," she said.

"Right, right, Miss Doyle," he said, quickly.

"And all I'm looking for is a cold beer," she said. "Is that all right with you?"

"That's fine, just fine, Ma'am," he said. "Enjoy."

The bartender hurried to the other end of the bar.

As the level of the conversations rose again, she realized that—in some corners—she was the subject. She just hoped all they would do is talk about her while she had her beer, and that no one would approach her.

But that was too much to ask.

She could feel men in the room getting up the courage to approach her. They were either going to try to get her into bed, or get her to go for her gun. She decided that her abrupt decision to have a beer was probably not a good one. She drained the mug, and turned to leave, but it was too late.

There was a man standing between her and the doors.

"Where ya goin', honey?" he asked. He was tall, in his thirties, wore a gun as if he knew how to use it. There was a smile on his face that said he usually got what he wanted. It just remained to be seen what that was.

"To my hotel," she said. "Move out of my way, please."

"Don't be in such a hurry," the man said. "Look, everybody here knows what you did in the circus. We're just wondering about your reputation, you know? I mean, so you can shoot at cards and glass balls. Can you shoot a man, or is that part of your reputation made up?"

"You don't want to find out," Roxy said. "Believe me."

"Well no," he said, "that's where you're wrong. See, my name is Mel Tatum, and Mel Tatum is nothin' if not curious. I've got to know everything." He laughed, looked around at his friends, three or four of them, who also laughed.

"Mel," the bartender said, "not in here."

"Shut up, Burt," Tatum said. "You served her, you kept her in here. We all talked about it, and now we're curious. And guess what? I got picked to find out."

"You didn't get picked," one of his friends shouted, "you picked yourself."

"So what do you want to do?" Roxy asked. "Shoot targets with me?"

"No, not targets, lady," Tatum said. "I wanna see if you're who they say you are. If you're who you say you are."

"Tatum—" she started, then stopped. She looked around the room. "If he's got friends here, talk him out of this."

"Ain't no talkin' him outta anythin', lady," somebody yelled.

"So show us what ya got, Lady Gunsmith!"

"Yeah, show us."

Suddenly, the entire saloon was chanting, "Show us! Show us! Show us!"

Roxy did what Clint Adams had told her never to do. She drew her gun on a man without meaning to kill him.

Tatum was totally shocked when Roxy drew and fired, and the holster went flying off his hip before he could even touch his gun.

The chanting stopped, and everybody stared.

Somebody said, "Jesus!"

Tatum looked down at his hip, his mouth agape.

Roxy pointed her gun at him.

"Your gun's on the floor, Tatum," she said. "Pick it up."

"Wha—hell, no," he said. "You just . . . shot it off my hip."

"That's right. I guess you wanted me to kill you, though. So pick it up and let's do it."

Tatum covered his mouth with his hand, then turned and stumbled out of the saloon. They could hear him puking on the street.

When the batwing doors opened it was Sheriff Marks and Deputy Andy who came in.

"What the hell is goin' on?" Marks demanded.

"Nothing," Roxy said, holstering her gun. That was another thing the Gunsmith had told her not to do. Do not holster your gun until you've replaced the spent round or rounds.

"What's wrong with Tatum?" Marks demanded.

"He came this close to gettin' killed, that's what's wrong with him," Burt the bartender said. "Jesus, I never saw nothin' so fast. She shot his holster right off his hip before he had a chance to touch his gun."

Marks looked down, saw the holstered gun lying on the floor.

"He wanted a fight, Sheriff," someone yelled. "She coulda killed him, but she didn't."

Andy bent down and picked up the holster and gun, stared at it, then looked at Roxy.

"That was some shootin'," he said.

"Can I go?" she asked. "I was on my way to my hotel when he challenged me."

"Yeah," Marks said, "that's a good idea. Go to your hotel. I'll talk to you later."

Roxy nodded, and walked outside, where Tatum was still bent over, emptying out.

He saw her looking at him, and gasped, "Thanks for not killin' me."

"You're a stupid sonofabitch!" she swore at him, and walked across the street.

Chapter Thirty

Roxy went right to her room.

She sat on the bed, removed her boots, her gun belt, replaced the spent round before hanging it on the bed post. Then she hung her head and took a deep breath. She could have easily killed Tatum. In fact, she was tempted to. Was she wasting her time with this circus business? Was it keeping her from finding her father? Was it dulling her senses, her instincts? Should she have killed that drunk?

No. Working for the circus was going to give her enough money to fund her search for her father for months.

Killing that idiot Tatum would have been a waste of time, and a bullet.

She was right in both circumstances.

When the knock came at her door she was tempted to ignore it, but then it became a pounding. She grabbed her gun and went to see who it was.

"Sheriff Marks!" he yelled from the other side.

She opened the door.

"What do you want?"

"To talk," he said, "and you won't need the gun."

She backed into the room, replaced the gun in its holster, then turned to face him.

"Leave the door open," she said, as he started to close it.

"Okay," he said, shrugging and leaving the door. "Tell me want happened."

"Didn't they tell you in the saloon?"

"Yeah, but I want to hear it from you."

She explained about going into the saloon for a beer, thinking it was a mistake, turning to leave and seeing Tatum in her way.

"He was an idiot," she said. "I could have killed him, but I didn't."

"You shot the holster off his hip," Marks said.

"Yes."

"What made you think to do that?"

"I did it tonight at the circus, with Bill Weatherly," she explained. "It seemed to be a way I could avoid killing Tatum."

"Well, I appreciate that," Marks said. "I mean, I know he's an idiot, but thanks for not killin' him."

"Keep him away from me," she said.

"Don't worry," Marks said. "I spoke with him. He wants nothin' to do with you. You really impressed him."

"It wasn't my intention to impress an idiot," she said.

"No, I can see that," he said. "Can you tell me how much longer you'll be in town?"

"However long the circus will be here."

"Will you be in this room?"

"They're supposed to have a wagon I can move into tomorrow."

"Okay, that's good," Marks said. "None of these other idiots will be able to get to you, then."

"No," Roxy said, "they won't."

"All right," Marks said. "I'll let you get some sleep."

"Thank you."

He stepped out into the hall, then asked, "Do you want me to close the door?"

"Yes."

He nodded, then closed it. She could hear him walking down the hall.

It was still early, but she found that she was tired. If she went to sleep now, she'd be up very early. She could check out and move to the circus. Hopefully, Jill would have that wagon for her.

She took off her pants.

***

In front of the hotel Deputy Andy was waiting for Sheriff Marks to come out.

"Is she in there?" he asked.

"Yeah, she's there," Marks said. "She's goin' to sleep."

"What should we do?"

"Nothin'," Marks said. "She didn't kill anybody, and what she did she was pushed into."

"What about Tatum's friends?" Andy asked. "What if they try to get at her tonight."

"Good point," Marks said. "Andy, you stay on her."

"Sir?"

"Keep an eye on her door, don't let anyone near it. "

"But . . . I have to go home."

"No," Marks said, "you have to do your job. Stay here, watch her door, don't let anyone near it. Got it?"

"I've got it."

"Good. I'll see you in the mornin'."

"I have to stay here all night?"

"All night," Marks said. "All right?"

"All right!"

Andy turned to go into the hotel, when Marks called out to him.

"Yeah?"

"I'll stop by your house and tell your wife."

"Okay," Andy said, "thanks."

Chapter Thirty-One

Roxy laid on the bed, wondering why she couldn't fall asleep? All she could think was that the hour was too early for her body. She didn't often turn in this early in the evening. She thought about pulling on her boots and going out again, but she'd had enough trouble for one day.

She walked to the window and looked down at the street, wishing her father would just ride in and end her search for dad.

She was about to return to the bed when she heard something. She stopped, and listened. Definitely the creaking of the floorboards in the hall outside her room. Grabbing her gun from the holster on the bedpost, she moved to the door and pressed her ear to it.

Definitely.

Holding her gun in her right hand, she reached for the doorknob with her left, turned it slowly, and then jerked the door open. She stuck the gun out ahead of her, jabbing it right into the midsection of Deputy Andy.

"Oof!" he said.

"What the hell—" she pulled the gun back, but reached out, hooked her fingers into his belt and pulled him into the room, snapping, "Get in here!"

He staggered into the room, and she slammed the door.

"What the hell are you doing creeping around outside my room?" she demanded.

"I'm doin' my job," he said. "The sheriff told me to keep an eye on you, and not let anybody near your room. I started down in the lobby, but then thought maybe I should come up and stay in the hall. How'd you know I was here?"

"Because you sound like a herd of cattle out there," she complained.

She walked to the bedpost and holstered her gun, then turned to face him. God, he was so young and fresh-faced, almost pretty. He'd grow into a handsome man.

"Suppose you tell me what you were really doing out there in the hall?" she asked.

"Whatayou mean?"

"Did you have your ear to the door?" she asked. "Did you think I might be in here with a man?"

"Wha—no, of course not! You're a lady, why would you have a man in your room?"

"You're in here," she pointed out.

"Yeah, well," he said, "I should go back out—"

"And besides," she said, moving closer to him, "I'm not exactly a lady."

"You are to me."

"That's sweet."

She kept walking until she was right in front of him. Then he grabbed her and came in for a kiss. She made it open-mouthed and probing, and at one point sucked his tongue into her mouth. It went on for a while.

She broke the kiss eventually and stepped back from him, leaving him breathing hard.

"I'm so sorry . . ." he gasped. "I just . . . couldn't help myself . . ."

"That was good, wasn't it?" she asked.

"You know it was," he gasped. "But you also know I'm married."

"Well," she said, "your wife's not here, is she?"

Abruptly, she pulled her shirt from her pants and unbuttoned it. Her full breasts came into view, and he couldn't help but stare. She knew the effect she had on men, and this young one was no different.

She moved closer to him again and reached down to cup his crotch. She could feel the hardness there.

"Impressive," she said, rubbing her hand over him.

"Don't—" he started, but she was already undoing his trousers. She dropped his gunbelt to the floor, then stuck her hand into his pants and grabbed his hard cock.

This was why she couldn't sleep. The session she'd had with John Steel hadn't completely satisfied her. Maybe this young bull could tire her out.

She yanked him toward the bed and, with a groan of surrender, he followed . . .

Chapter Thirty-Two

She stripped him and pushed him down on the bed, then finished undressing herself. Her intention was to take her time with this one, and not get it over with quickly, as she had with Steel. She just hoped the deputy was up to it.

She got on the bed with him and began to kiss his smooth, hairless body. His skin was soft, and he smelled good. He was only a couple of years younger than she was, but he seemed much more. She knew he was less experienced, from his reactions to her.

As she kissed and stroked him, he had no idea what to do with his hands.

"Put your hands on me," she told him. "Touch my skin."

"Like this?" he asked.

"No," she said, "stroke me, feel me, squeeze me," she said. "Like this." She took his cock in her hand and squeezed it.

"Jesus!" he said.

"Don't worry," she said, "you're not going to shoot off yet."

"How do you know?"

She smiled. "I'm not going to let you."

She squeezed his cock again, then got down between his legs and began to lick him.

"What are you doin'?" he asked.

"Doesn't your wife do this?" she asked.

"N-no."

"Or this?" She took him into her mouth.

"Jesus, no!" he said. "Don't w-whores do that?"

She released him and smiled up at him.

"There's a little whore in all women," she said. "Didn't you know that?"

"N-no," he said. "I-I'm not very experienced."

She kissed his belly. "That's very brave of you to admit." She kissed his thighs. "I guarantee you that after tonight, you'll be more experienced." Once again she took him into her mouth, and began to suck . . .

***

Later, after she allowed him to explode into her mouth, she stroked him to fullness again and mounted him, taking him into her hot pussy.

"Oh God," he said.

"Just relax," she told him. "Let Roxy do all the work."

She began to move on him, sliding up and down his pole, enjoying the way he felt inside of her. And she liked his body. Young and strong. His wife was lucky, she got a good one. She felt bad for a moment for tempting him, taking him down the wrong path, making his cheat. But then she felt the tremors starting in her belly, her legs, and forgot all about that. Closing her eyes she floated . . .

Later still she made him climb atop her, jam it in and fuck her hard.

"Come on, harder, harder . . ." she cried out. "Doesn't your wife like it hard?"

"No," he said, through clenched teeth, "she likes it soft and slow . . ."

"Well, there's a time for that," she admitted, "but right now I want it hard. Come on . . ." she dug her nails into his back, ". . . do it hard!"

***

She was finally exhausted, and thought she could sleep. He was lying on his back next to her. She slapped him on the belly, and he came awake.

"Time for you to go," she said. "I need some sleep."

"Huh? Oh, yeah," he said. "Sure."

He stood up and got dressed.

"And why don't you just sit down in the lobby?" she suggested. "Instead of creeping around outside my door, huh? I might shoot you by accident."

"Sure, okay."

He was glum, no smiles at all. She knew that was because he was feeling guilty.

"Hey," she said, from the bed.

He turned and looked at her, stared at her naked body, then looked away.

"Don't feel guilty," she told him. "I pretty much forced you."

"I could've said no," he said. "I just don't know what I'm gonna tell my wife."

"Nothing," she said. "If you're smart you won't tell her a thing."

He shook his head. "She's gonna know, as soon as I walk in, she's gonna know."

"Give it a chance," she said. "She won't know a thing if you just take it easy."

He went to the door.

"And remember," she called after him, "it was my fault not yours."

"Yeah," he said, "sure."

She rolled over in bed, feeling guilty only for as long as it took her to fall asleep.

Chapter Thirty-Three

Roxy woke to a pounding on her door. Gun in hand, she went to answer it.

"Who is it?" she asked, standing off to the side in case somebody decided to fire through it.

"It's Jill! Come on, open up!"

Roxy opened it a crack, saw Jill, and then pulled it wide. Slowly she turned and walked to the bed, where she sat.

"What time is it?"

"Eight a.m.," Jill said, entering and closing the door. "Whew! I can tell from the smell in here what you were doing last night. Good for you!"

Roxy put the gun down and rubbed her face vigorously with both hands.

"Who was it? Was it that John Steel? The gambler? He had a nice smile. Or somebody else?"

"Nobody you know," Roxy said.

"Well, come on, get dressed," Jill said. "I got a wagon and I had it cleaned. It isn't going to smell like this room. Whew! I mean, unless you have company."

"Yeah, okay," Roxy said. "I'm ready to check out."

As she sat there she became aware that Jill was staring. Roxy's legs were bare, and the blouse she was wearing left little to the imagination, especially her large nipples, which were poking out from it.

"Jill?"

"Hmm?"

"You want to wait for me in the lobby?"

"Really?"

Roxy got up, took Jill's arm and led her to the door and out into the hall.

"Okay, okay," Jill said, "I get it. You're modest. I'll be downstairs."

Roxy closed the door.

***

She came down to the lobby with her saddlebags and rifle in hand, Jill was sitting on a wicker chair against one wall. When she saw Roxy she stood up and joined her at the desk.

"Checking out," Roxy said.

"So soon?" the clerk asked, wistfully.

"She got a better offer," Jill told him.

The man glared at her, and took Roxy's money.

"Okay," she said, "let's go."

"Let me carry those for you," Jill said, taking the saddle-bags.

"Thanks."

Outside on the boardwalk the two of them walking together drew stares. Jill ignored them; Roxy was only watching in case somebody drew a gun.

"You want to do some shopping?" Jill asked.

"For what?"

"New things. What else does a woman shop for?"

"Why do I need new things?"

"You've got a pocketful of money," Jill said. "Isn't it burning a hole?"

"No," Roxy said. "That money's going to help me find my father. And maybe buy a box of bullets."

"Oh my God," Jill said, "am I going to have you teach you how to shop?"

"No," Roxy said, "no shopping."

"You're going to need some new clothes for the act," Jill said. "You've seen how Bill dresses."

"Yeah," Roxy said, "buckskins."

"They're expensive buckskins," Jill pointed out.

"Jill," Roxy said, "I'm not buying a bunch of fancy clothes."

"They don't have to be so fancy," Jill said, "just something that will help you stand out—like your hair."

"What's wrong with my hair?"

"Nothing," Jill said, "it's something special. I just want your clothes to match your hair."

Roxy thought about it for a moment, then asked, "So where do we go?"

***

They stopped at the mercantile to pick up a few new shirts for Roxy, things that Jill said would go with her hair. When they reached the circus ground Jill was carrying the packages, while Roxy was once again carrying her saddle-bags and rifle.

They walked across the grounds back to the area where all the wagons were, and Jill led the way to the one that would be Roxy's for as long as she was with the circus.

"Here you go," Jill said, opening the door. "After you."

Roxy stepped into the wagon, set her saddlebags and rifle down. Jill came in behind her, put the packages down on the bed—which was more of a pallet than anything else.

"So, what do you think?"

"It's fine," Roxy said. It was a little smaller than Bill Weatherly's wagon, but had the same setup, and smelled better, since Jill said it had been cleaned.

"Fine?" Jill asked.

"I mean, it'll do," Roxy said.

"It's one of the best wagons we have," Jill told her.

"I appreciate it," Roxy assured her.

Jill wasn't getting the reaction she had expected, and gave up.

"All right, then," she said, "you might as well get yourself relaxed. I'll check in on you later."

"Okay."

Jill headed for the door, then stopped.

"Do you have a rehearsal with Bill today?"

"I don't think so," Roxy said, "We pretty much have the routine worked out."

"It did go well last night," Jill said, "I was just hoping for . . ."

"What?"

"Oh, for something more . . . flashy, I guess," Jill said, "but that's just me. The crowd loved it."

"Yes, they did," Roxy said.

"So, okay then," Jill said, "we're all set."

"When are we pulling out for Denver?" Roxy asked.

"We've got a performance tonight, and a matinee tomorrow, then we'll take the rest of the day to break everything down and be on our way."

"Okay."

"In a hurry to get going?"

"If my father's not here," Roxy said, "there's really no point in staying. I was also told he might be going to Denver, so . . ."

"Well, for all our sakes, I hope that's right," Jill said.

"Why for all our sakes?"

"If he shows up here in the next day or so, you probably won't go to Denver with us. And if he shows up in Denver, you'll be happy. And I want you to be happy." Jill patted Roxy on the shoulder. "See you later."

"Thanks," Roxy said, then waved her arm, "for this."

"Hey," Jill said, "you're one of our headliners."

Jill left, and Roxy sat on the pallet in the dark wagon, thinking she should light the lantern.

But she didn't.

***

Lester the Clown watched as Jill left the wagon and headed back to the center of the circus grounds. Now he knew where Roxy Doyle would be when she wasn't out in front of a crowd.

His next step was figuring out how to kill her while she was in that wagon.

Chapter Thirty-Four

Eventually, Roxy lit the lamp and tore open the brown paper packages holding her new shirts. They were way too loud for her taste, but Jill told her they'd be perfect for performing.

She actually found the little wagon kind of cozy. All she needed was some beef jerky and a bottle of whiskey so she could snack occasionally, and have a drink after performing. Maybe even a few cans of peaches. For that she'd have to go back to the mercantile.

She left the wagon, started to walk away, but then spotted Weatherly's wagon. Jill's question of rehearsal was in her head, so she walked over and knocked.

"Hey!" Weatherly said, opening his door a crack. "How are you?"

"Fine," she said. "Jill just showed me to my wagon, over there." She pointed.

"That's good," Weatherly said, still not opening the door wider than a crack. But through that crack Roxy thought she could see skin.

"Oh, sorry," she said, "you're not alone, are you?"

"No, I'm not," he said. "Uh, we can talk later, all right?"

"Bill," a tiny voice said from behind him, "I'm waitin'."

At first Roxy was shocked. It sounded like a little girl, but then she knew why.

It was Kiki, the little clown.

"Okay, yeah," she said, suddenly embarrassed. "Later."

"Thanks," he said, and closed the door.

Roxy stood there staring at the closed door, and listening. Suddenly, she heard a high-pitched laugh from inside, and backed away quickly. She looked around, hoping no one had seen her.

She couldn't help but wonder what the tableau inside looked like. Weatherly was a big man, and Kiki was so small.

She walked away, shaking her head at the appetites of some people.

***

She was in the mercantile, picking out her items, when she saw a woman and a small boy enter the store.

Deputy Andy's wife and son. She had only seen them once at breakfast, but recognized them.

Suddenly, for the second time that day, she felt embarrassed. But they were between her and the door, so she couldn't get out. She decided to just continue shopping.

Deputy Andy's wife exchanged a greeting with the store clerk, who then leaned down and handed the little boy a piece of candy.

"What do you say?" Mrs. Starrett said.

"Thank you," the boy replied.

"I was takin' care of this lady," the clerk said, indicating Roxy.

"That's okay," Roxy said, "I can wait."

"Thank you," the woman said to Roxy.

"All right then, Mrs. Starrett, what can I get . . .."

"You're pretty."

Roxy looked down at the little boy, who was staring at her with big eyes.

"Why, thank you," she said.

"I like your hair."

She put her hand on his head and said, "I like your hair, too."

"My dad's a deputy."

"Is that right? You must be real proud of him."

"I am," the boy said. "He puts bad guys in jail."

"I'll bet he's very good at it," she said.

"That's enough, Sam," the boy's mother said. She had a bundle in her arms. "Leave the lady alone. We have to go."

"He wasn't bothering me," Roxy said.

"He doesn't need to talk to you," the woman said, coldly. tugging the little boy toward the door.

Jesus, Roxy thought, does she know? Did the deputy tell her, after all?

"Don't feel bad," the clerk said. "That woman doesn't like anybody."

"Really?"

"Oh yeah," he said, "especially not another pretty woman."

"She is kind of pretty," Roxy said, thinking it was in a faded way.

"Not as pretty as you," he said, "and for that reason, I'm sure she really hates you."

Well, if that was the reason, Roxy could live with it.

"Thank you," she said to him, "I needed that."

The clerk looked confused.

"I'll take a few cans of peaches," she started, "and . . ."

Chapter Thirty-Five

Lester the Clown looked around, didn't see anyone in the area, opened the back door of the wagon and went inside. This was one of the supply wagons for the circus. Everything they needed to break down or erect their circus was in there. He'd checked the other two wagons already. He hoped to find what he needed, and get away without being noticed.

He wasn't actually Lester the Clown now, he was just Les Collier. He figured he'd have a better chance of going unnoticed that way.

He rummaged around in the wagon for a few minutes before he finally found what he wanted. The carton was sealed. He found a crowbar, used it to carefully pry open the carton. He took out two sticks of dynamite, then sealed the carton again, slamming the nails back home with a nearby hammer. He hoped two sticks would not be missed.

He opened the door to the wagon a crack, looked out, then wider so his head would fit. When he didn't see anybody lurking, he stepped out, closed the door, and hurried away.

What he didn't see was Coco the Clown.

***

Coco the Clown was curious about Lester. Coco had been a clown for over 10 years. He'd been with Pomerantz for 6. Lester had been with them only a few weeks, and Coco didn't like him. He thought Lester was one of those people who was using the circus to hide. Then, when they arrived in Blackhawk, he started acting funny—especially when Roxy Doyle showed up. So Coco decided to follow Lester, and see if he could figure out what was going on.

He saw Lester go into all three supply wagons, and finally come out with something in his hand. Now all he needed to figure out was what was in that wagon that could be carried away in one hand.

And why did Lester need it?

***

Roxy went back to her wagon and stowed away the peaches, beef jerky, and whiskey. That done she decided to clean her guns, make sure they were in proper working order for the show, and in general.

She was just finishing, putting her gun down when a knock came at the door. She picked it up again and answered it.

"Who is it?"

"Lulu Mae."

She opened the door. The bearded lady held up a bottle of champagne and two tin cups.

"Welcome to the neighborhood."

"Come on in."

She backed up, let the other woman enter. Lulu Mae was wearing a form fitting blue dress that accentuated her curves.

Roxy assumed that was how she dressed when she was a "freak on display".

They sat down at the table and Lulu Mae poured, handed Roxy a cup. They clinked cups and drank.

"Rosita would've come, but she couldn't fit in here with us."

"That's okay," Roxy said. "You're all the company I need—unless you wanted to bring Kiki."

Lulu Mae laughed and said, "Yeah, she'd fit just fine."

"I went to Bill Weatherly's wagon a little while ago, to talk about our act?"

"Yeah?"

"He had somebody with him."

"Really? Must be a repeat offender. We don't have any new girls—except you."

"Well, from the sound of her voice I think it was Kiki."

Lulu Mae sat back.

"Ah, little Kiki's gettin' some more."

"What about her and Coco? Do they get along?"

"I'm sure they do," Lulu Mae said. "They're the only little people with the circus, and they are married."

"What would Coco do if he found out about Kiki and Bill?" Roxy asked.

"Well, first we don't know if he already knows," Lulu Mae said, "and second, probably nothin'. Bein' in a circus, or a carny family, is different from other families."

"You mean you share everything?"

Lulu Mae laughed again.

"Pretty much."

144

"I don't know I can live that way."

"Nobody says you have to," Lulu Mae said. "If you find a man you like, keep him for yourself. But you better be sure he thinks the same way."

"I'll keep that in mind."

"Might start with Coco."

"Why's that?" Roxy asked, amused by the suggestion.

"According to Kiki," Lulu Mae said. "He really well hung."

"I'll keep that in mind," Roxy said, "although I don't think I'm that curious. Have you . . ."

"No, not me," Lulu Mae said. "Not yet, anyway. But you know? I'm getting more and more . . . experimental."

She stood up to leave. "You keep the bottle, and welcome aboard."

"Thanks, Lulu Mae."

"Now that you're in the family," Lulu Mae said, "just call me Lu."

"I will."

She walked Lu to the door and watched as she stepped out. Then when she tried to close it, it wouldn't latch and lock. She tried again a couple of times, with no success. She finally decided she had to go and find Jill and tell her, because Roxy couldn't very well leave it unlocked all the time.

She got her hat, stepped out of the wagon, tried to close the door several times again, then got frustrated and slammed it.

The explosion drove her off her feet . . .

Chapter Thirty-Six

She opened her eyes and sat up quickly, then groaned.

"Take it easy!"

She put her hand to her head, which hurt like hell, then looked to see who was speaking. It was Jill.

"Where am I?" she asked. "What happened?"

"You're in my wagon," Jill said. "Yours blew up, and you got knocked out. Lulu Mae was there and ran for help. I had some of the men carry you in here."

"Jesus . . . my ears are ringing."

"From the explosion, no doubt. It destroyed your wagon. And right after I had it cleaned."

Roxy tried to sit up, but Jill held her down with a hand on each shoulder.

"I sent someone for the doctor, and the sheriff," she said. "Just lie back and relax."

"The sheriff?" Roxy asked. "I thought circus people handled their own business?"

"Not this," Jill said. "Somebody tried to kill you."

"For the second time," a man said.

Roxy became aware that someone else was there when Bill Weatherly came into view.

"You want to tell her, or should I?" Weatherly asked.

"Tell me what?" Jill asked.

"Someone took a shot at us," Roxy said. "At me."

"When?" Jill asked.

"Yesterday, when we came out of Bill's wagon to go and rehearse."

"We weren't sure who the target was, but I guess we are now," Weatherly said. "Jesus, somebody tried to blow you up with dynamite."

"Where'd they get the dynamite from?" Roxy asked.

"We have some in one of our supply tents," Jill said. "They probably got it there."

A knock came at the door, then, and Jill let the doctor in. There were a bunch of people gathered outside.

The doctor, who looked somewhere between 60 and 80, said, "Can you step out please while I examine her?"

"We'll be right outside," Jill said. "A lot of our people are out there, wanting to know if you're all right."

"Why?" Roxy asked, her ears still ringing.

"You're part of our family, now," Jill said.

She and Weatherly stepped out of the wagon, and the doctor began his examination . . .

***

"Well," he said, later, "you've got a bump on the head. I'm assuming that was from a piece of flying debris, possibly even the door."

"And the ringing in my ears?"

"That'll go away," he assured her.

"Anything else?"

"I don't see anything else," the doctor said, putting his jacket back on. "You'll probably have headaches for a while. If you need something for the pain come and see me."

"Okay," she said. "Thanks, Doc."

He nodded, opened the door and stepped out. Roxy caught a glimpse of a crowd outside, then Jill and Weatherly stepped back in.

"What did he say?" Jill asked.

"I'm fine," Roxy said, swinging her feet to the floor of the wagon. "I'll have a headache for a while, and the ringing in my ears will go away. Oh, and the bump on the head, probably when the door flew off the wagon."

"The door?"

"It wouldn't lock," Roxy said. "I slammed it, and then the wagon exploded."

"Wow," Jill said, "if you hadn't slammed it from the outside . . ."

"Right," Roxy said, "I'd be dead. Apparently, not everyone is welcoming me into your little circus family."

***

The next knock on the door came from the sheriff and, behind him, his deputy.

"Is she all right?" Andy asked, when Jill opened the door.

"She's fine, Deputy," Jill said.

Sheriff Marks stepped into the wagon, then turned and blocked Andy's path.

"Not much room in here, Andy," he said. "Why don't you stay out there and question some of the people, see what they saw."

"Yes, sir."

Marks closed the door in Andy's face, then turned to look at Roxy.

"How are you feelin'?" he asked.

"Blown up."

"Any idea who did it?"

"Not yet."

"What's that mean?"

"This is the second attempt on my life," Roxy said. "And I'm going to find out who's behind it."

"Second? Why haven't I heard about this?"

"I was keeping it to myself so the shooter would be off balance."

"So the first was just a shot?" Marks said. "He sure has graduated. What's gonna come after dynamite?"

"Nothing," Roxy said, "because I'm going to find him, first."

"We all are," Weatherly said.

Marks looked at him and Jill.

"We don't like having anybody blow up our wagons," Jill said, "or our people."

"Especially not with our own supplies."

"So he used your dynamite?"

"He must have," Roxy said, "unless he bought it in town."

"I'll check with the mercantile, but I don't even know if he carries explosives."

"One of the other businesses in town might have some," Weatherly said.

"But it makes more sense that whoever it was got it here, from our wagon," Jill said.

"Fine," Marks said, "so we'll all be checking." He looked at Roxy. "If anythin' else happens, don't keep it to yourself this time. Let me know."

"I'll be sure to tell you," Roxy said, "or your young deputy."

"You do that," Marks said.

He left the wagon.

"We need to find you a new wagon," Jill said, frustrated, "but you can share this one with me until then."

"Why not?" Roxy asked. "I don't have anything left that will take up space. Just my horse and saddle, in the livery, the clothes on my back, and the gun on my hip."

Jill smiled. "Looks like you'll have to go shopping, again."

***

After the doctor and lawmen left, outside the wagon a few of the circus family were still lingering. Lulu Mae and Rosita were there. So were Kiki and Coco, and some of the other clowns—including Lester.

Lester was damning his luck that the dynamite he had planted underneath Roxy Doyle's wagon had gone off before he was ready. He didn't know if he could get away with stealing more from the circus supply wagon. There would probably be a guard on it, after this.

He decided to walk away, before someone wondered why he was still hanging around.

***

"Why are we still here?" Kiki asked Coco.

"Because he is," Coco said, indicating Lester.

They were not in their clown guises. Kiki was under four feet tall, busty, with pale skin and blonde hair. Coco was just over four feet, with red hair and large hands. At the moment, he was stroking his chin.

"What's he got to do with anything?" Kiki asked.

"That's what I'd like to find out," Coco said.

"Well not me," Kiki said. "I've got other things to do."

She walked off, leaving her husband staring at Jill's wagon.

Chapter Thirty-Seven

Jill and Weatherly left to find Roxy a new wagon. Roxy remained in the wagon, waiting for her headache to abate, and the ringing in her ears to subside.

About twenty minutes went by. She was lying on her back on Jill's bed when there was a knock at the door. She got up and walked to the door, still wearing her gun.

"Who is it?" she asked, trying to stand as far to the side as she could.

"It's Coco, the clown."

Coco?

She opened the door. The little man looked up at her with a broad smile.

"Hello, Miss Doyle. We ain't really met yet. I'm Coco."

"Yes, I figured that," she said. "Up to now I've only seen you in full make-up."

"Can I come in?"

"What's this about?"

"It may be about who blew up your wagon."

"Okay," she said, "come on in."

He stepped in and moved past her. She looked around outside, then closed the door.

"Where's Kiki?" she asked.

"I don't know," he said. "She might be in Bill Weatherly's wagon, bouncing up and down on his cock."

"You know about that?"

"I know Bill," he said, "and I know Kiki. The rest wasn't hard to figure out."

Roxy sat down at the table, which put her on more level terms with Coco, who remained standing.

"What's on your mind, Coco?"

"Well, you are."

"I don't understand."

"Come on," he said, "you're a woman, I'm a man."

"Oh," she said, surprised.

"Okay, I know I'm small," he said, "but in one way I'm big—real big. I mean, like a third leg big."

"Oh," she said, again.

"Ask any of the women around here," he said. "Ask Kiki."

"Coco—"

"Look," he said, "you're the most beautiful thing I've ever seen. I really want to be with you. What do I have to do to make that happen? I'll do anything."

"Coco," she said, "I'm really flattered—"

". . . but you'd rather be with Bill Weatherly," he said. "I get it."

"I haven't been with Bill Weatherly," she said, "and I don't intend to be."

"Why?"

"Well, for one thing, he's married. I don't sleep with married men. And second, he doesn't appeal to me."

"What about me?" he asked. "Does my offer appeal to you? Look, I can show you." His hands went to his belt.

"No, no," she said. she found herself . . . curious . . . but said, "You don't have to show me. Look, you're married."

He dropped his hands.

"So that's the reason?"

"That's it."

"You won't be with me, and you won't be with Weatherly."

"No."

"Well," he said, "that sort of makes him and me equal, don't it?"

"In my eyes," she said. "Yes."

"So, like, even kissing is out?"

"Out," she said.

"Well, whataya know," he said.

"What about Kiki?" Roxy asked. "Aren't you mad that she's been with him?"

"It makes her feel equal to the other women he's been with," Coco said. "I'm glad for her. It gives her some confidence."

"I guess I see." She thought she did. Being with a regular sized person made them feel accepted. She wished she could help Coco out, but she really didn't think she could go through with it.

"Was there anything else you wanted to say to me?" she asked him.

"Well," he said, "I was gonna trade this for a night in your bed, but since that's out, I guess I'll just give it to you."

"What is it?"

"You know Lester the Clown?"

"No, I haven't met him, yet."

"Well, he ain't' really a clown. He joined us a few weeks ago when we came across him on the road, carrying his saddle. Jill hired him because we were short one clown. See, Bobo died."

"That's too bad."

"Well, he was old."

"Okay."

"He's hiding from somebody, or something," Coco said. "That's why he wears his clown make-up almost all the time."

"I guess that's a good way to hide," she said. "Why did you think I'd be interested in this information? Do you think there's a bounty on him?" Could her father have been hunting this clown-who-wasn't-a-clown, and that's what was bringing him to Blackhawk?

"Well, he kinda creeps around here, and I've taken to following him, sometimes. I was following him today when he went through the supply wagon."

"The supply—are you telling me he set the dynamite on my wagon?"

"Now," Coco said, his big hands waving about in front of him, "I didn't actually see him do that. But I saw him come out of the third wagon carrying something."

"What was it?"

"Something he was able to hold in one hand."

Dynamite, she wondered. One or two sticks?

"Anything else?"

"He was hanging while we were waiting to hear if you were all right."

"What's his real name?"

"Les Collier."

"Do you know where he is now?"

"No."

"Can you tell me what he looks like?"

"Well, he's got orange hair—"

"No," she said, "I mean, what he really looks like?"

"Yeah, that's what I'm telling you," Coco said. "He's got kind of orange hair, you know, red, but it looks orange? Other than that, he's kinda . . . normal looking."

"And as Lester?"

"Lots of orange hair," he said. "You can't miss him. "He's the only one of us with hair that orange, black around the eyes, and wide, red smile painted on, even though I don't think I've ever seen him smile."

"Coco, I really appreciate this." She leaned forward and kissed him on the cheek.

He touched the spot with his right hand, then held the hand out to her.

"Have you seen my hands?"

"I have."

"Pretty big, huh?"

"They're big," she admitted.

"You know, they say big hands, big—"

"Thanks so much Coco," she said, standing. She towered over him.

"Oh, sure."

They went to the door and she let him out. From what she could see, no one was milling about, anymore. And she didn't see a man or a clown with orange hair.

Chapter Thirty-Eight

Roxy left the circus grounds. She didn't want to go looking for Lester the Clown just yet. First, she walked back to town to the sheriff's office. Marks was surprised when she walked in

"So soon?" he asked. "What can I do for you?"

"Does the name Les Collier mean anything to you?"

"Les Collier," he repeated, then shook his head. "No, why?"

"Do you think you might have a wanted flier on him?"

"I can look," he said. "What's this about?"

"He's with the circus performing as Lester the Clown," She said. "I've been told he may be hiding from something."

"Like a bounty hunter?"

"Maybe."

"Huh." Marks thought a moment. "Sounds like a good place to hide."

"If he's hiding from my father, and he knows I'm with the circus now—"

"I think I see where you're goin'," Marks said. "Maybe he thinks you're workin' with your father, and he's the one who tried to shoot you, and then blow you up."

"That's what I'm thinking."

"Okay," Sheriff Marks said, "I'll have Andy go through our posters and see what he comes up with. Are you gonna brace this clown?"

"Not yet," she said. "I don't want him to know I'm onto him."

"He may try again."

"I'll be ready for him," she assured him.

"All right," Marks said, "if Andy finds him on a poster I'll send him over."

"All right, thanks."

"Don't mention it," Marks said. "The fact is, I don't like havin' people get blown up in my town—especially beautiful girls."

"I'll see you, Sheriff." She started for the door, then stopped. "Oh, did you find out anything about someone buying dynamite?"

"Didn't happen," he said. "Not in this town."

"Thanks."

She left his office. Maybe it was time to go and talk to Lester the Clown, but first the person who hired him.

Jill Weatherly.

***

"Roxy!"

She had looked for Jill back at her wagon. Not finding her she went to the tent with the food and coffee, and there she was.

"Hello, Jill."

"How are you feeling?"

"I'm fine. I'm going to get some coffee. You want a refill?"

159

"Yes, thank you." Jill gave Roxy her cup.

When Roxy returned to the table she set Jill's cup down in front of her and sat across the table.

"Tell me about Les Collier."

"Who?"

"Lester the Clown."

"Oh, right," she said. "That is his name, isn't it? Well, what do you want to know?"

"Why did you hire him?"

"We needed a clown, and he needed a job."

"And a place to hide."

"Maybe," Jill said. "I don't usually ask too many questions. But I'm sure there are few people here hiding from . . . something."

"I'm only interested in Lester."

"Why?" she asked. "Oh, wait, do you think he—Lester the Clown?"

"He was seen coming out of a supply wagon carrying something in his hand."

"Dynamite?"

"Not sure."

"Who saw him?"

"Coco."

"What?"

"He came to me, tried to trade what he knew for some time in bed with me."

Jill's eyebrows went up.

"Did you do it?"

"No," she said, "but he told me, anyway."

"Why?"

"I assured him I don't sleep with married men," Roxy said. Not him, and not Bill."

"Ah, so you put them on equal footing."

"I did."

"You missed out."

"You've been there?"

"Oh, yes," Jill said. "Sorry, I was curious."

"One time?"

"One time."

"Was he telling the truth?"

"About what?"

"A third leg."

"Oh yeah," Jill said. "I couldn't walk straight for a week—but it was worth it."

Chapter Thirty-Nine

Nobody knew where Lester was.

Roxy walked around the entire circus, which was in full swing, with locals coming and going. The show in the big tent would be starting soon, but she and Weatherly weren't set to go on for hours.

She questioned some of the clowns, but they didn't know that much about Lester.

"He keeps to himself," said a clown named Fuzzy, who had fuzzy purple hair.

Finally, she got to Kiki, who was in her wagon, applying make-up. Roxy was able to see what a pretty face she had as she was doing it.

"Lester?" she asked. "No, he doesn't talk very much, not to me, or Coco. You talk to the others?"

"I did," Roxy said. "They said the same thing."

"Well, obviously he's hidin' from somethin'."

"Seems like it. Thanks."

"Did my husband tell you about him?"

"Yes, he did."

Kiki smiled. It made her even prettier.

"Did he try to make a trade?"

"He did, but I didn't."

"Good for you. I knew he would, as soon as you started working here. You're so pretty."

"You're pretty," Roxy said.

"Yeah, but you're beautiful . . . and normal. Coco likes 'em normal-sized."

"Don't you?"

Kiki turned back to her mirror.

"You're talkin about Bill Weatherly."

"Is he the only one?" Roxy asked.

"No, but lately, yeah. Okay, so I like 'em normal-sized, too. There's nothin' wrong with that."

"I didn't say there was. Thanks for talking to me."

She started to leave the wagon.

"Hey, Roxy."

"Yeah?" Roxy turned.

"You missed out."

"So I've been told," Roxy said. "I'll just have to try and live with it."

Kiki laughed and went back to her mirror.

***

Roxy took one more walk around the grounds. She was looking for Lester's orange hair, and was still keeping her eyes peeled for Gavin Doyle.

As it got late in the day she got hungry, stopped by the food tent. Both Lulu Mae and Rosita were there.

"Hey, honey," Lu said. "Over here."

Roxy took her plate over to their table to join them. She sat next to Lu, across from Rosita.

"You looked tired, hon," Rosita said. "You gettin' enough to eat?"

Roxy looked at Rosita's plate, only there wasn't just one, there were three.

"Plenty," Roxy said, "but I've been looking for Lester all day."

"Lester the Clown?" Lu asked. "Why him?"

"I think he's the one who tried to blow me up," she answered.

"Lester?" Lu asked.

"Why not?" Rosita asked. "We don't know him that well."

"True," Lu said, "but that's circus people hurtin' circus people.

"It's been done before," Rosita said. She looked down at her three empty plates for something to eat.

"I heard a word the other day that I don't know the meaning of," Roxy said, remembering.

"What was it?" Lu asked.

"Rube," Roxy said. "What does it mean?"

"'Rube,'" Lu said, "has a few meanings. Sometimes we use it to describe folks who aren't circus people."

"Inexperienced people," Rosita said.

"In the old days it was somebody who watched a tent, made sure nothin' happened to it," Lu went on. "But mostly it's used when there's a fight brewing."

"If a circus or carnival person needs help," Rosita said, "they yell "Hey, Rube,' and everybody's supposed to come runnin'."

"I get it," Roxy said.

"So if you ever need help while you're part of our circus," Lu said, "if Lester or anybody else tries to hurt you, you just yell 'Hey, Rube,' and we'll all come runnin'."

"Well," Rosita said, laughing, "I'll come a-runnin' as fast as I can."

The three women laughed.

"So you can't find Lester?" Lu asked.

"Not since the explosion."

"Maybe he left," Rosita suggested.

"I hope not," Roxy said. "I haven't let it be known that I suspect him."

"But you been askin' around about him," Lu said.

"Well, yeah . . ."

"Then he probably got the word," Rosita said.

Roxy thought a moment, then said, "Damn."

Chapter Forty

If Les Collier—also known as "Lester the Clown"—was gone, then it was her own fault. On the one hand, that was bad, because she wouldn't be able to make him pay for trying to kill her. On the other hand, it was good, because he wouldn't be trying to kill her, anymore. She didn't know which she preferred.

But there was a third eventuality. If Les Collier was once again on the move, and Gavin Doyle was on his trail, then the bounty hunter would not be coming to Blackhawk.

Roxy felt she'd been in Blackhawk enough days to determine whether or not her father was going to show. The thing about the rumors were they were more often than not untrue. She constantly heard rumors that Wild Bill Hickok was alive, the Gunsmith was dead, Lady Gunsmith was dead, and Gavin Doyle was dead. So far, she knew for sure that three of those were just flat out lies. Didn't it then make sense that the fourth one was, as well? She certainly couldn't even consider that her father was dead, or else what had she been doing these past 10 years since leaving Utah?

Jill found Roxy wandering around the grounds.

"They're about ready for you and Bill," she said.

"That's fine," Roxy said. "I'm ready, too."

"I was hoping you'd be wearing one of your new shirts, but I guess that's impossible now, thanks to Lester," Jill said, as they headed for the big tent.

"I didn't have time to shop again," Roxy told her. "I've been busy."

"I know," Jill said, "trying to stay alive and find the guy who tried to kill you. Not to mention your father."

"Yeah," Roxy said, "all that."

"What About Denver?" Jill asked. "You still committed to going with us?"

"I told you I would," Roxy said, "I'll keep my word, but I don't know what's going to happen after that."

"Fair enough," Jill said. They reached the tent and saw Bill Weatherly waiting for Roxy. "Good luck," Jill said.

"Luck's got nothing to do with it," Roxy assured her.

***

The routine went perfectly that night, and again the next day at the matinee. After that, they began to break the circus down for the trip to Denver. Wagons were loaded, the lions were in their cages, Roxy was still sharing Jill's wagon, which could have made it a bit uncomfortable that night, sleeping wise. However, Jill decided to let Roxy have the run of the place, and went to spend the night with her husband in his private wagon.

"I thought he slept here with you?" Roxy commented.

"Some nights," Jill said. "It depends . . . on a lot of things."

But apparently there was nothing keeping Jill from her husband's private wagon, that night.

Roxy was amazed at the speed with which the circus roustabouts broke the tents down. By the time they were done they still had several hours of daylight. Rather than wait for the next morning, they were going to pull out immediately, get some miles in before camping.

They rode through town one last time, with people lining the streets, applauding and waving as they waved back. Roxy rode her horse at the head of the procession with Bill Weatherly, who waved with his hat. At one point Roxy saw Mrs. Andy with her little boy, and while the tyke was waving and laughing, the wife was staring daggers at her. If she didn't know better, she would have thought that the wife was behind the attempts on her life.

As they came to the end of town Roxy saw Sheriff Marks on the sideline. He waved at her to come over.

"Found your Les Collier on a poster," he told her. "Wanted in six states for robbery, and in one state for murder."

"Thanks, Sheriff. It looks like I missed him, but I appreciate the information."

"Good luck to ya," he said, tipping his hat.

He wasn't such a bad guy, after all.

Chapter Forty-One

Denver, Colorado

Fifty miles and four days later, they arrived in Denver. The circus traveled at a speed just exceeding that of the old wagon trains that traveled westward.

They stopped in a field outside the city. Astride her horse, Roxy could see the city spread out before them. Jill came walking up alongside.

"What are we doing all the way out here?" Roxy asked.

"Well, the fact is we ain't P.T. Barnum or Buffalo Bill Cody," Jill said. "The big arenas won't take us, so we've got to set up where we can. But don't worry, the people will come out to see you and Bill shoot at each other."

Jill turned and walked back to the wagons, started shouting out orders to the roustabouts, pointing where to erect what.

Roxy turned in the saddle to examine the mountains around them. She'd been feeling that they were being followed for days. It could have been Les Collier, still aiming to make a try for her, or it could have been bandits meaning to rob them. It could also have been some renegade Indians who strayed off the reservation. If it was Indians, though, she wouldn't have felt them. You never knew Indians were about until they fell on you. She learned that when her mother was killed on the wagon train her family had taken west sixteen years before.

Or there might have been no one there, at all . . .

***

Les Collier looked down on the circus wagons as they began to disgorge their contents. The roustabouts set to erecting tents and displays. From his elevated position, he could see Roxy Doyle. She was easy to spot, with that red hair, and that body of hers.

If he was a good enough marksman he could have taken her off that horse with one shot, but he'd missed his shot when he was a lot closer, atop one of the wagons. Now that he was hundreds of yards away, he had no chance. He had to get closer.

Collier thought about just riding away when he left the circus, but then he'd still have to worry about bounty hunters and Roxy Doyle. A woman like Lady Gunsmith wasn't about to forget that somebody tried to kill her, and by now she had to be certain it was him.

His best bet was to wait until the circus was up and running, and the grounds were full of spectators. Then he could get closer to her and make a killing shot.

He had "Lester the Clown" in his saddlebags. He'd be invisible on the grounds as just another clown. By the time somebody spotted him and recognized him, the job would be done and he'd be on his way.

Then no more Lester the Clown, and no more Lady Gunsmith.

***

Jill had decided that she and her husband had to move into his private wagon, so that Roxy could have hers. Bill Weatherly wasn't real happy about it, but he was going to have to find someplace else to take his various women. Jill knew that lately he'd been sleeping with little Kiki, and since she had once had sex with Coco, she didn't mind. It was all in the family.

But she didn't want to be there to watch it, so he was going to have to take little Kiki somewhere else.

Since she and Bill were sharing the wagon, she figured they might as well share other things—like the bed.

She sat astride him with his long hard cock buried deep inside of her, and rode him up and down. She wondered how he could fit that thing into Kiki's pussy, but she still wasn't curious enough to watch.

From the hardness of his penis inside her, she knew that he was perfectly capable of satisfying them both.

She rode him until her entire body was a quivering mass of pleasure, and then fell atop him, her head on his chest.

"Oh baby . . ." she said.

"You are somethin', honey."

"Better than all your other women, baby?"

"Now, you know none of them means anythin' to me, sweetie. You're my wife. They're just circus folks."

"Part of the family."

"Right."

"And what about Roxy?" Jill asked. "Have you been with her, yet?"

"Roxy? No, there's nothin' between me and Roxy except our act. We bring emotions into the act, and one of us would end up dead."

"Just keep that in mind?" Jill said. "Roxy's mine."

"You been with her yet?"

"No, not yet," Jill said, "but she's softening."

"Now that," Weatherly said, "I'd like to watch."

"No chance," Jill said, looking up at him. "You're not gonna watch me, and I'm not gonna watch you and Kiki."

"Kiki," he said, in a soft voice.

Jill sat up and stared down at her husband.

"Say that again."

"Say what again?"

"Say 'Kiki,' again."

"Kiki."

"No, say it the way you just said it," Jill told him.

"How do you mean?"

"I mean, say her name like you love her."

"Kiki?" he said. "Love her? You're crazy. I love you, Jill. And Kiki's married. She's with Coco."

"And you're married," Jill said. "You're with me." She moved her hips so she could get her hand down between his legs, and grabbed his balls. "You remember that."

He grunted as she squeezed. "I'll remember it, honey."

"That's good," Jill said, releasing her hold. "That's very good."

She climbed off him and started dressing. He watched her long, lean body disappear beneath her clothes, was surprised that he didn't feel the sense of loss he usually felt when he watched her get dressed. Could she have been right about him and Kiki?

"I've got work to do," Jill said, smoothing down the front of her shirt.

"Does that mean finding Roxy a wagon?"

"That's part of it," Jill said. "But I also have to choose who's going into Denver to drum up some business."

"That's easy," he said, sitting up.

"Oh yeah? Well, you tell me who to send and I'll tell Pomerantz."

"There's only one person everyone's gonna want to see," he told her. "Lady Gunsmith."

"Not you?"

"No, not me," he said, grabbing his pants. "Not yet, anyway."

"Then when?"

"Right after I kill Lady Gunsmith in a fair fight," he said, "they'll all be coming around."

Chapter Forty-Two

"What the hell are you talking about?"

"I'm talking about outdrawing Lady Gunsmith."

"You can't outdraw her," Jill said.

"Hey, remember, I've performed with her now three times. I know I can beat 'er."

"And why would you want to?"

"Are you kiddin'?" he said. "Do you know how many people would flock to this show to see the man who killed Lady Gunsmith?"

"That's . . ." She was going to say crazy, but changed it. ". . . genius."

"Yeah, it is."

"But how would you avoid the law?"

"Because it'll happen as part of the show," he said. "Like I accidentally outdrew her and killed her. No jury would convict me. And if it does go to trial, that'll get the word to even more people."

"What about her father? Won't he come after you?"

"Come on," he said. "He's dead, everybody knows that."

"Everybody but Roxy."

"Right."

He was dressed now, and standing next to her.

"When are you going to do it?" she asked. "First night?"

"The first night we have a big crowd," he said. "I want enough people to leave here talkin' about it, and spreadin' the word."

"You know," she said, putting her arms around him, "you're a pretty smart man."

***

Roxy decided to pitch in and help the roustabouts, which wasn't appreciated by some of the other performers.

"Honey," Rosita said, pulling her aside, "they're roustabouts, we're performers. There's a difference . . ."

". . . a divide . . ." Lulu Mae added.

". . . that you don't want to cross."

"I was just kind of bored sitting around doing nothing," Roxy said.

"Also," Lulu Mae said, "the roustabouts don't like being around your gun."

"They're afraid they're gonna get shot," Rosita said.

"Oh."

"Anyway," Lulu Mae said, "Jill and Pomerantz have called a meeting. They're deciding who's going to be parading into town."

Roxy gave in, let go of the rope she was holding, and followed the other two "performers."

***

"Roxy," Jill said, "we're gonna want you and Bill to ride up front. Is that okay?"

"That's fine," she said.

She had already assigned all the others who were going to be hanging out of wagons, waving at what was hopefully an appreciative crowd. She had also given the job of putting up posters to some of the roustabouts and clowns.

"Shit," Coco said, "we never get to go into town." He walked away.

"Why is that?" Roxy asked.

Kiki looked at her. "We're too short." She raised her hands. "We can't put them up high enough. Makes sense to me, but it always bothers Coco."

Roxy was thinking she wouldn't have minded riding into town and putting up some posters. It would enable her to see a lot of Denver, and keep an eye out for her father, or Collier.

As for riding out in front, it made her a perfect target for anybody with a grudge or a desire for a reputation, but she couldn't very well hide in the shadows.

She was learning about being a carny.

Chapter Forty-Three

The ride through Denver seemed to be a success.

Crowds turned out, lining the streets. Even Market Street, a major thoroughfare, was mobbed. The Pomerantz Circus may not have been Buffalo Bill Cody's Wild West Show, but maybe next time they wouldn't have to set up in a field outside of town.

Of course, Jill told Roxy she was the draw. Next time, if Roxy wasn't there, these people would stay at home, or at work.

When they returned to the field to set up for the next day's opening, something bothered her. If she was the draw, and her father was around, then he knew where she was. She'd wondered all these years if he knew she was looking for him. Surely, word would have gotten around. So why hadn't he come looking for her?

Because he was dead?

***

Roxy's new wagon was larger than the one before.

"If I was you," Jill said, handing her the key, "I'd check underneath it every night."

"Understood," Roxy said.

"Want me to come in and help you try it out?"

That was more brazen a comment than Jill had been using up to now. Roxy wondered why?

"That's okay, Jill," Roxy said. "I've got it."

"Well, take somebody inside with you," Jill said. "Bill, Coco . . . Lu . . . somebody! It'll loosen you up."

Loosen her up? Did she seem as tense as she felt? Did everyone sense it?

She went to the new wagon, checked underneath it, and then went inside.

When she got inside and turned on the lamp she almost drew her gun. Coco was there, on the bed, naked, his vaunted third leg on display.

He stroked it and said, "I just wanted you to see what you're missing."

"Get out!" she shouted. "I almost shot you."

"Okay, okay," he said, scrambling off the bed and into his clown pants. A regular pair of pants would not have been able to accommodate that erection. "Jeez, it would help you, ya know? You're too tense."

As he went out the door she said aloud, "Why is everyone saying that?"

***

She knew she was tense.

It wasn't because she was going to be performing in front of a crowd 5 times the size of the ones in Blackhawk.

It wasn't because she was waiting for Les Collier to make another try at killing her.

It wasn't because she needed sex. She had Steel and Deputy Andy in the past week.

Good God, she thought, it's because I'm thinking my father doesn't want to see me, or he's really dead.

Had he been hiding from her all these years?

Or had he been killed years ago?

She didn't know which eventuality would be better for her. But really, she did.

Neither.

She had to continue to believe that he was alive and out there, somewhere. She had to continue to follow up on rumors. Why would there be all these rumors if he was dead. The fact that they existed in such abundance had to indicate he was alive.

That's the way she chose to read the situation, and that was the inspiration for the way she would continue to live her life.

For now.

Chapter Forty-Four

The next day the grounds were mobbed.

Lulu Mae, Rosita, Kiki and Coco, all the performers, the "freaks," were on display and working hard.

Roxy walked around the grounds, people recognized her and pointed. They even shouted at her.

"Lookin' forward to seein' you shoot, Lady Gunsmith."

"Rootin' for you to beat the men!"

"Give 'em hell, Roxy!"

The sharpshooting competition was being advertised, again, and people were signing up to take on Roxy and Bill Weatherly. Both men and women were shouting out to her, but from the line of them waiting to talk to Jill and sign their names, the competitors were all men.

"Never had this many before." She turned, saw Bill Weatherly behind her.

"It's you," he told her. "They all want to compete with you."

"And you," she said.

"Naw," he said, "they couldn't care less about me. It's Lady Gunsmith they want. And that's okay. Jill and Derek are gonna make a bundle on this, and that's what's important."

He walked away.

Roxy couldn't believe that Bill Weatherly wasn't bothered more than that. The fact that he bedded as many women as he did, meant that he did indeed, have an ego. So what was behind this display of modesty?

Tired of the shouts directed to her—even though most of them were encouraging—Roxy decided to get something to eat before the show.

When she reached the tent it was empty, as almost everyone involved with the circus was working. There was a pot of beef stew bubbling away, seemingly untouched as of yet. She filled a bowl and took it, with a cup of water, to a table.

***

Les Collier did not even have to become "Lester the Clown" in order to be hidden amongst the crowd on the circus grounds. In his trail clothes he was able to blend in very nicely.

But as thick as the crowd was for him to hide in, it also kept him from finding Roxy Doyle, so he knew he was going to have to go where the rubes couldn't go—behind the scenes—to locate Lady Gunsmith and put a bullet into her.

Or he could wait until her show with Bill Weatherly, shoot her and disappear into the crowd. Everyone would think she had accidently been killed by the circus sharpshooter.

Okay, that sounded like the more logical course of action. But that meant he had to buy a ticket. Luckily, he had spent most of his time in the circus as "Lester the Clown," and he was sure there weren't that many people who knew what he really looked like, beyond Jill Weatherly and, maybe, Derek

Pomerantz. A simple ticket seller was not going to recognize him.

He decided to give it a try. Buy a ticket and if the seller didn't say, "Hey, ain't you Lester the Clown?" then he'd be in the clear.

He made his way through the crowd to get in line for a ticket . . .

***

Roxy was finishing her beef stew when the only other circus performer who wasn't busy at that moment came walking over—Bill Weatherly.

"Bill," she called, "join me. The stew is very good."

He walked over to the table, but came away only with a cup of coffee, and joined Roxy.

"I can't eat before a performance," he confided. "But after, I'm famished."

"Don't tell me you feel nerves before?" she asked.

"I do," he said. "It has nothing to do with my ability with a gun. It's the crowd that gets to me. And this will easily be the biggest crowd we play to—probably until tomorrow."

"Tomorrow?"

"Well," he said, "after these people return home, and go to work tomorrow, and pass the word . . . well, tomorrow's crowd will test the stitches in our big top, I'm sure."

"That's interesting," Roxy said.

"How are you feeling?" he asked.

"Me? I have no nerves when it comes to the performance."

"I mean, after the attempts on your life."

"These weren't the first attempts and they won't be the last," she said. "And Les Collier seems to have lit out for parts unknown, so I'm fine. If I was going to worry about that, I wouldn't have ridden out in front with you when we went to town."

"I wondered about that," Weatherly said. "I mean, if there'd be a shot from the crowd. Thankfully, there wasn't. I was ready to come to your defense."

"Thank you, I appreciate that."

He nodded, sipped his coffee. She noticed, when he looked at her, that there was none of the shades of lust or desire she'd seen in the eyes of most men.

"Can I ask you something?"

"Sure."

"I don't want you to misunderstand," she said. "I'm not saying I want to sleep with you."

"Of course not."

"Why haven't you tried?"

"You've heard all the stories about me," he said.

"Yes. I was just wondering if it's because of Jill."

"Jill? No. Oh, she's my wife, but she doesn't care if I sleep around. But . . ."

"But?"

"She'd be upset if she found out that I had . . . feelings for another woman."

"And do you?"

183

"I'm afraid I do," he said, "and I don't know how to handle them. It's never happened to me before."

"Really? And who is it? Can I ask?"

"You can," Weatherly said. "It's Kiki."

"Kiki? Really? You're in love with Kiki?"

He put his coffee cup down and stared into it. "I guess I am. Sounds odd, don't it? And I don't mean because she's . . . little. That really doesn't matter to me. She's a fine woman. No, I think it sounds odd because I never would have expected it to happen, not with any woman."

"And is she in love with you?"

"I think so."

"But you're both married to other circus people," Roxy said. "What will you do?"

"I don't know, and that's the problem," he said. "I don't know how to handle this."

"Well," Roxy said, "I hope it's not going to be on your mind during our routine?"

He smiled. "Don't worry about that. I don't take my personal life under the big top with me."

"That's good to hear."

"Just as you obviously don't."

"No, I don't."

"Well then," he said, standing up, "if you're finished eating I guess we ought to be getting over to the big tent. Fritz the Ringmaster will probably be calling our names very soon."

They had to get over to the tent and get ready, which meant donning those extra holsters Weatherly kept so they could shoot them off of each other.

She fed the last morsel of stew into her mouth, stood, and said, "I'm ready."

Chapter Forty-Five

Before the night's performance Jill called a meeting of the clowns. She talked for ten minutes, and then asked, "does everybody understand?"

"We got it, boss," Coco said.

"Good. Let's put on a show."

The clowns ran out as the ringmaster, Fritz, began making his announcements. He told the crowd that while the sharpshooters would be performing the next two nights, on the third day they would be having the sharpshooting competition, where the first prize was $500. The crowd went wild.

"We know you've been enjoying yourselves so far, but here are our headliners—sharpshooters Bill Weatherly and Roxy Doyle, otherwise known as . . . Lady Gunsmith!"

The crowd went even wilder as Weatherly and Roxy came out, Weatherly doffing his hat and bowing.

They did some trick shooting, and then lined up on their marks for their shootout . . .

***

In the crowd, Les Collier was ready with his gun in hand. He was leaning next to one of the stands, so that he wouldn't fire his gun while there were people all around him. He knew he could shoot right from there, and then run out of the tent and get lost in the crowd outside.

And this time, he wasn't going to miss.

***

Weatherly and Roxy were intent on each other—that is, on each other's holster, which is where their shots were going to go.

The clowns were still bustling around, but as the time drew nearer for Roxy and Bill to draw, even they stopped to watch—except for Kiki and Coco.

Coco got behind Les Collier, and Kiki in front of him. For as hidden away as he thought he was, the two little clowns had spotted him as soon as he entered the tent.

As Weatherly and Roxy prepared to fire, Coco spoke from behind Collier.

"Hey, Lester, what's goin' on?"

Collier turned and looked at Coco.

Kiki ran out behind Roxy and said, "Behind you, Lady Gunsmith!"

***

Roxy was so intent on what she was doing that she still drew first, shot the holster off Weatherly's hip, felt the holster fly from her hips, and then turned.

She saw where Kiki was pointing, and there was a man somehow tripping over Coco, who was rolling into the back of his knees.

"That's Lester!" Kiki shouted to Roxy.

187

Roxy took off running as the crowd exploded and Weatherly took a bow.

When she reached Collier he was getting back to his feet, gun still in his hand.

"Stand right there, Lester!"

He froze in mid-crouch, and Coco rolled away from the action.

"What the hell did I ever do to you?" she asked.

He didn't bother trying to deny it.

"You're a Doyle," he said, and brought the gun up.

Since her holster had been shot from her hip, she still had her gun in her hand, and simply raised it and shot him. The bullet hit him in the chest and put him flat on his back.

Roxy ran to him, as did Kiki and Coco.

"He's dead," Coco said, looking at Roxy. He was in full clown regalia, but she could recognize his eyes.

"He said he tried to kill you because you're a Doyle?" Kiki asked.

"He's wanted," she said, "and he thought I was a bounty hunter." She stood up. "How did you spot him in this crowd?"

"Our eye level is different from everyone else's," Coco said. "And Kiki knows shoes."

"I spotted his worn boots," she said. "They're the only pair he has. He even wore them when he was Lester."

Jill and Pomerantz came running over.

"Is that Lester?" Pomerantz asked.

"It was," Roxy said.

"Why don't you go out and take your bows with Bill," Jill suggested. "We'll move the body and send for the law."

"Right," Roxy said. "Thanks."

She ran out to stand next to Weatherly as the crowd continued to cheer.

"You okay?"

"I'm fine," she said, "now."

Chapter Forty-Six

The Denver police wanted to know everything. Roxy told them that Les Collier was wanted. They said they'd check it out. If he was, indeed, wanted, and there was a bounty, did she want it?

No!

She wasn't a bounty hunter. That was her father, Gavin Doyle, she told them.

"I thought he was dead," the detective said.

***

Roxy got herself a cup of coffee and sat at the table with Lulu Mae and Rosita.

"Is it over?" Lu asked.

"Mostly," Roxy said. "The police just have to confirm that Les was wanted."

"You gonna get a bounty?" Rosita asked.

"No," Roxy said, "but I should probably tell them to give it to Kiki and Coco. They saved my butt."

"Here comes Kiki now," Lu said. "You should tell her."

Roxy turned and saw the pretty little blonde coming towards them.

"We should talk," Roxy said.

"That's what I was comin' to say," Kiki said. "Alone."

"Excuse us," Rosita said, and she and Lu left the table.

"The police wanted to know if there was a bounty did I want it," Roxy said "I don't. How about you and Coco?"

Kiki shrugged. "I'll ask my husband, and see what he says."

"Okay." Kiki didn't seem too thrilled with the extra money.

"I heard you had a talk with Bill," she said, "about him and me."

"That's right."

"And he told you we were in love?"

"Yes. Was that not right?"

"It's about half right," Kiki said. "He's in love with me, but I was just havin' some fun. I don't wanna leave my husband, Roxy."

"Did you tell Bill that?"

"No," she said. "Not yet." She bit her lip.

"What is it?"

Kiki's pale little hands were dry washing each other furiously.

"What else is on your mind, Kiki?" Roxy asked.

"There's somethin' I got to tell you, Roxy," she said, "and I wish I didn't, but . . ."

Chapter Forty-Seven

Bill Weatherly was right.

The next night the crowd was noticeably larger. They were not only there for the phony shootout, but because they heard that Lady Gunsmith had killed someone the night before.

Could it happen again?

***

Jill came up alongside Roxy while she and Weatherly were waiting to go on.

"All set?" she asked.

"Oh, yeah," Roxy said. "I'm ready." She turned her head and looked Jill right in the eye. "For anything."

Jill blinked several times, opened her mouth to say something, but then Fritz called for Roxy and Weatherly to come out and she stepped aside.

"This is my last night on the job, Jill," Roxy said, turning her head. "I quit."

"Let's give 'em a great show tonight," Weatherly said, smiling.

"Is that what you call it?" Roxy asked.

"Call what?" he said, still smiling for the crowd.

"Planning on killing me in front of all these people."

His smile almost slipped.

"What?"

"You know what I mean."

"Who told you? Jill?"

"Oh, no," Roxy said. "Jill's very loyal to you. But I found out. What I can't figure out is why you think you can do it. You said yourself you're not a fast draw act."

He looked directly at her, now, and lost his smile.

"I said I wasn't a fast draw act," he said, "not that I wasn't a fast draw."

"But don't forget," she told him, "you've never shot at another person—especially not one who was shooting back. You thought you could kill me because I'd be shooting at your holster. Well, guess again."

That seemed to faze him.

They went through their paces, shooting targets that were being held or thrown by girls and/or clowns. But when it came time for them to face-off, the crowd got quiet.

Roxy wondered if Weatherly was having second thoughts about trying to kill her? She knew she couldn't take that chance. But she really didn't want to kill him, so she knew she was going to have to go against all her training, and try something special.

As they stood face-to-face, she kept eyes on his shoulders, so as to gauge his move. When it came, she knew she had him beat easily. She could've killed him with no trouble. Instead, she shot his holster off his hip.

While his gun was still in it!

Understanding that she was faster than he realized, and could have killed him, he went along with the act. Turning, he played to the crowd as if he was shocked at what had happened—which he was.

***

Outside the tent Roxy didn't even bother heading for her wagon. She wanted to get off the circus grounds as soon as possible, go to a hotel. In the morning she'd buy a new set of saddlebags, and a rifle with her new-found fortune of $500, and be on her way. She just wasn't sure to where.

***

She was saddling her horse when Kiki came walking up to her.

"Jill's lookin' for you," she said. "I think she wants to thank you for not killin' Bill."

"And you?"

"Me? He's not my husband. I'm kinda glad you scared the wits out of him. That was some shootin'."

"Thanks."

"Where are you off to?"

"Don't know," Roxy said. "Denver, I guess, for a short time. I need to get outfitted, and take the time to look for my father."

"And if he's not there? It's just another rumor?"

"Then I move on to the next one."

"The next town?"

Roxy mounted, looked down at Kiki and said, "Next rumor."

Coming Spring 2018

Lady Gunsmith 5
The Portrait of Gavin Doyle

For more information
visit: www.speakingvolumes.us

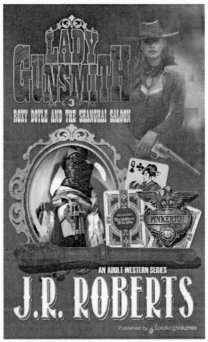

Now Available

Lady Gunsmith 2
A New Adult Western Series

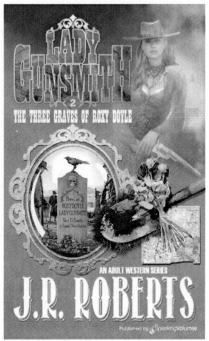

Here Lies Roxy Doyle, Lady Gunsmith
shot to death in Sunset, New Mexico.

By
AWARD-WINNING AUTHOR
J.R. Roberts

For more information
visit: www.speakingvolumes.us

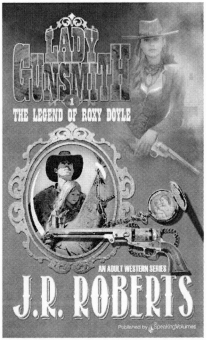

Now Available

TRACKER *series*
by
Award-Winning Author
Robert J. Randisi (J.R. Roberts)

Visit us at www.speakingvolumes.us

Now Available

MOUNTAIN JACK PIKE *series*
by
Award-Winning Author
Robert J. Randisi (J.R. Roberts)

Visit us at www.speakingvolumes.us